When the summer tourists depart for home
and the sunshine wanes,
a deep, dark quiet descends on this coastal town.
And the children begin to learn about the night . . .

Taggard Point
THE FOREVER HOUSE

There's one hollow, boarded-up house on
Maitland Road all the teenagers know not to
go into, even on a supreme dare. But that rule
is about to be broken . . . *forever.*

THIS BOOK ALSO CONTAINS A PREVIEW OF
THE NEXT TERRIFYING
TAGGARD POINT NOVEL . . .

Shapes

Coming in May from Berkley Books

Taggard Point

Book 1

The Forever House

Mark Rivers

B

BERKLEY BOOKS, NEW YORK

THE FOREVER HOUSE

A Berkley Book / published by arrangement with
the author

PRINTING HISTORY
Berkley edition / February 1995

ISBN: 0-425-14567-0

BERKLEY®
Berkley Books are published by The Berkley Publishing Group,
200 Madison Avenue, New York, New York 10016.
BERKLEY and the "B" design
are trademarks belonging to Berkley Publishing Corporation.

PRINTED IN THE UNITED STATES OF AMERICA

10 9 8 7 6 5 4 3 2 1

This one's for Devan,
because he's Devan,
good enough reason.

And for Matt,
because he's Devan's father,
and a good friend.

1

Amy Lowell sat on the top step of her front porch on Oakwood Street and waited for the world to end.

If it had, she wouldn't have been surprised.

For some reason, it seemed that somewhere along the line, when she wasn't looking, somebody had changed her middle name to "Misery." Or, if there really was such a thing as paying for the bad stuff you did in a past life, she must have been Attila the Hun.

First there was her name. Every one of her teachers, practically from kindergarten, reminded her at least thirty times a day that she shared the same name with a poet who had been dead for a zillion years, maybe more. Her high school English teachers were the worst; one had even made her write an essay about it.

Next was her face. She had black curly hair, fair skin, a decent if slightly pudgy figure, pleasant smile, and . . . freckles. Not many; just enough sprayed lightly across her nose to make all her aunts and uncles pinch her cheeks and tell her, constantly, how darling she was, how cute, how . . . adorable.

With only six weeks to go until she reached sixteen, adorable was not exactly what she hoped she looked like.

Then there was today.

She, Becky Savage, and Spike Amanti had been hanging out over in Conner Park in the center of town, goofing around with a water balloon, threatening one another with it, ducking around a gnarled oak and laughing, just enjoying the summer-warm, September afternoon. Everything had been fine, until she had spotted her father walking toward them.

Before she could stop herself, she had a plan.

Moments later, she and Spike were hiding in the branches, while Becky wandered around below, sup- posedly acting as lookout. The foliage on the old tree was thick, not yet turning, so they couldn't see very well, and the shouts and laughter from a nearby softball game prevented them from hearing Becky's promised signal.

So when a man finally walked under their branch and paused, Spike immediately dropped the balloon. They burst into hysterical giggles, and Sergeant Frank Silver looked up and snapped, "You! Down! Now!"

He wasn't amused.

After that, it was a stern lecture from the policeman, a not-quite-but-almost-smiling lecture from her father, and the threat of a grounding she figured would probably last until she graduated from Beachland High. If not longer.

It wasn't as if she'd never been in trouble before. She had been. The trouble was, she kept coming up with these plans for jokes, and explorations, and experiments, and adventures, none of which were horrible or dangerous, but almost all of which ended in disaster.

Her parents called it Fate; her friends nicknamed her "Net." For "Magnet." As in the trouble that always seemed to be attracted to her, even when she wasn't involved.

Not anymore though, she vowed as she swiped invisible dust from her jeans. From now on she would hold her tongue whenever an idea struck. Let someone else come up with the brilliant schemes and complicated plans. The new Amy Lowell would be a follower, not a leader.

If nothing else, it would keep her mother from strangling her.

A sharp nod to her shadow sealed the bargain, and crossed fingers hoped she'd be able to keep it.

Someone called her then, and she waved when she saw Becky hurrying up the sidewalk.

Her best friend was slender and still tan, today in T-shirt, sneakers, and cutoff jeans. Her nearly white-blond hair was pulled back in a ponytail that flopped lazily against her spine when she walked.

"You okay?" she said, stepping around the low hedge that bordered the Lowell homestead.

Amy grunted.

"I tried to tell you."

Amy mock-glared at her. "You could've yelled or something, you know."

Becky's big blue eyes widened innocently. "But then I would have gotten in trouble too."

"No kidding," she said miserably.

Becky grinned and plopped down on the bottom step. "Guess you're not going to the movies tonight, huh."

"Ha."

"Just wondering."

In silence they watched a convertible drift past, music blaring, a quartet of seniors sprawled on the seats. From the opposite direction a spotted dog trotted along the sidewalk, sniffing the edges of lawns, the trees at the curb, anything that struck its fancy while its wire-tail wagged furiously. A breeze drifted down from the painfully blue sky, bringing with it the tang of salt air from the ocean, six long blocks away. Another car sped by.

The neighborhood—tall trees and small brick homes and small front yards—was normal.

"Boy, it's like a graveyard around here," Becky complained mildly.

Maybe it was, but Amy didn't mind. She had been to Boston and New York, and had seen all the sights and the people and the shops and the hotels. It had been interesting and exciting, no question about it, but she had always been glad to get home to Taggard Point. Her hometown wasn't exactly tiny, but it wasn't huge either, and except for the flood of beach-bound tourists between Memorial Day and the end of September, it was, for the most part, fairly peaceful.

It suited her.

Becky, on the other hand, had major plans: graduate from Beachland High in two years, then go to college in California, study acting, and become a world-renowned movie star before she was twenty-one. The only time she would return to the Point would be for the premiere of her first motion picture at the Driftwood Theater.

Amy hadn't the slightest idea what she wanted to do.

Except maybe find a way to get rid of her stupid freckles.

"So what do you want to do?"

Amy looked down at her friend. "Like I have a choice?"

The girl grinned. "We could always go over to WonderLand and watch them take down the Ferris wheel."

Amy rolled her eyes. After a summer hanging out on the beach, the boardwalk, and the amusement-park pier, she didn't want to admit the fun season was really over. Watching the rides being prepared for the winter wasn't her idea of a good time.

It was depressing.

"So," Becky said, cupping her hands around her knees, "I saw Jon a while ago."

Amy didn't answer.

"He was heading this way."

She still didn't answer, but a curious tightness began to squeeze her chest.

"You think he heard about this afternoon?"

"Only if you told him," Amy answered sourly.

"Who? Me?"

Amy couldn't help it; she grinned. Becky had been trying to hook her up with Jon Vernon ever since school started three weeks ago. True, he was good-looking; true, he seemed to like the same things she did; and it was also true that he'd been sneaking glances at her every time she snuck glances at him. But that didn't mean anything. Not really. Besides—

"Hey, there he is." Becky's voice lowered. "Nuts. Spike's with him."

Amy took a deep breath, and casually ran her hands through her hair and straightened her T-shirt. Just in case.

The boys were on the other side of the street, both in jeans, high-tops, and shirts that hung over their belts, but Jon was a good head taller than Spike, and at least twenty muscled pounds heavier. All of it, she noted, in all the right places.

Becky waved them over.

Amy did her best not to squirm, especially when Jon grinned at her. "Nice work, Amy. Bombing the police in broad daylight. All the post offices in the country will have your picture right up there on top."

Spike laughed, but instantly shut up when he saw the look on her face. Jon, however, took the step just below her beside Becky, giving Amy a close look at the top of his head. She wanted to touch it. Then he leaned back against her knees, and she almost passed out, smiling stupidly when he tilted his head and looked at her upside down.

"I saw Dev this morning," he said quietly.

No one said a word.

Dev Costello's older brother had left home a year before without a word, without warning, two days after graduation. Nothing had been heard from him since, and neither the police nor his family had a clue what had happened. Amy knew Jon was fishing for news, and not doing it very well.

That was another thing she didn't like—Stan Lowell was managing editor of the *Point Dispatch*, and everyone figured she would get all the juicy details and inside information from her father before anyone else. Especially the stuff that never saw print. Sometimes it made her feel good; most of the time, it was just a pain.

She shook her head regretfully.

Jon sighed, but he didn't sit up.

Spike, who had dropped to sit cross-legged on the flagstone walk, clapped his hands once and rubbed his palms together. "So. What's the plan for tonight?"

Amy gave him a *thanks, pal, rub it in why don't you* look that made him grimace at his forgetfulness.

"Sorry, Net."

"No problem."

"Well, I have an idea," Jon announced casually, sticking out his legs and crossing them at the ankles.

Becky nudged him with a sharp elbow. "No ideas

allowed around here," she warned. "Remember who you're dealing with."

He laughed. "It's okay. I'm immune."

Amy rapped his head with a knuckle. "Right. Like the time you helped me with the frog in Mrs. Samson's desk."

A simple gag, harmless, and a good laugh in an otherwise stodgy biology class. Except that Mrs. Samson knew right away whose idea it had been from the way Jon kept flashing the okay sign to Amy. Both of them had ended up cleaning the lab for a week.

"No problem," he said with a grand wave of his arm. "This is so simple, not even Net could screw it up."

Amy wanted to hit him.

She did.

He yelped, scrambled to his feet, and stood with his hands on his hips. "Just for that, I'm not going to tell you."

"Good," Becky said. "It'll keep us out of jail."

But Spike grabbed him around the legs and begged him to tell. He tried so hard, Jon toppled onto the grass where they wrestled around for a few seconds, while Becky rolled her eyes.

"Boys," she said with disdain.

Amy agreed.

Finally Jon shoved Spike away and got to his knees. "Exploring," he said.

Amy remembered her vow and shook her head.

"Where?" Spike asked eagerly.

Jon smiled slowly and he lowered his voice. "Where else? Maitland Road."

No one smiled.

The breeze turned abruptly chilly.

"What's the matter?" he asked. "Don't tell me you guys are scared of a few haunted houses?"

Taggard Point had been founded in the mid-1700s on a lonely stretch of Atlantic coastline between a low, wooded hill and a narrow freshwater river. Scrub pine and oak had covered the rest of the land.

No one knows why Ethan Taggard had chosen this isolated place to settle his large family; no one knows exactly where he came from. Yet he cleared the land and laid out the streets and welcomed those ships that happened to pass by, carrying immigrants who couldn't find what they wanted in the other, more distant colonies.

There weren't many, but they came.

The Point struggled for nearly a century, until wealthy inland families decided it would be a nice place to visit, and to build summer homes for themselves and cottages for their servants. It wasn't long before the village became a town, and when, after the invention of the airplane, the rich found other, more exciting places to go, the Point built its boardwalk and aggressively sought the dollars of other summer tourists.

The carriages and servants were gone, but the old houses remained.

Many had changed hands several times, each new owner fixing and adding on, restoring and repainting. A few stayed in the possession of the descendants of the original families. Fewer still were bought and lived in, but only for a while before the owners, for one reason or another, moved quickly on, leaving no trace behind.

Maitland Road was three blocks in from the beach.

Maitland Road, where it met the steep, rocky slope of Storm Hill, had three old homes no one had occupied for over a decade.

And no one, not even the kids, had had the nerve to go inside.

Spike—whose real name was Oliver, though no one used it on pain of death or worse—stayed behind when Becky and Jon, after failing to convince the others of the brilliance of his idea, wandered off toward Tidal Row, the Point's extra-wide main street. He sprawled on the grass with a sigh, eyes closed, one hand cupped behind his head, the other in his pocket mindlessly jingling his change; it was a habit that drove all his friends up the wall.

Amy moved off the steps and sat beside him, knees drawn to her chest. "He's nuts."

"Sure he is."

"Those places are dangerous."

"Right."

"Everything's probably all rotted out inside."

"Sure."

"There's an elephant in the middle of the street."

"Yep."

She slapped his stomach hard, making him gasp and cough. "You're not listening to me!"

He opened one eye and grinned. "Every word. And you're right. You'd have to be an total idiot to go in one of those places."

She nodded, absently rubbing her bare arms as the breeze chilled her again.

"Hey," he said quietly.

She looked at him.

His eye closed again. "Sorry about before. At the park, I mean. It was my fault. You shouldn't have taken all the heat, you know?"

She shrugged. "No big deal. I'll live."

"You grounded?"

She wasn't sure. Usually, one of her father's lectures was punishment enough after one of her escapades—he had a voice that could bring down a redwood when he really got mad—but her mother had been in a bad mood lately, and there was no telling what she would do when she heard. Right now, she was at work, manager of a dress shop on Tidal Row, and she wouldn't be home for at least another hour.

"Tell you what—if you can bat those big eyes at your dad hard enough, maybe he'll let you out tonight." He shrugged. "Maybe I could . . . you know . . . make it up to you? A movie or something?"

Amy stared at him, a little surprised at the offer. Although she had known Spike most of her life, it had never occurred to her to date him. He was . . . well, *there*, that's all. A shoulder to cry on, someone to yell for help to when she got stuck in math, someone to hang out with. But always in groups. Seldom alone.

And she surprised herself by saying, "Sure. Okay."

His smile lasted so long she thought he'd fallen asleep.

Suddenly he sat up, winked at her, and pushed to his feet. He held out his hand, she took it, and let him pull her up. Which was how they were when her mother pulled into the driveway.

"Oh boy," she muttered.

Spike instantly dropped her hand and backed away across the lawn. "I'll call—"

"Young lady," said Vera Lowell, sliding out of the car.

"See you," Spike whispered.

"Young man," Mrs. Lowell added sharply.

Spike froze.

Amy managed a smile that was as bright as it was false. "Hi, Mom, what's up?"

Mrs. Lowell was as dark as her daughter, but considerably more round and a good six inches taller. When she leaned back against the car and folded her arms across her chest, Amy couldn't help thinking of a cop getting ready to take on a gang single-handedly.

"You two are going to be the death of me, you know that?"

Amy lowered her gaze and stared at the ground. This was not going to be good. She knew that tone. It usually meant doom.

"Mrs. Lowell," Spike said hastily, "don't blame Amy for what happened, okay? I'm the one who did it. Really!"

"Maybe so. But it was Amy's idea, am I right, Amy?"

She nodded meekly.

"I helped," Spike offered.

Then Amy heard something that made her look up, not sure she could believe either her eyes or her ears.

Her mother was laughing. She didn't want to, that much was clear, but her cheeks were flushed, her eyes were nearly shut, and the bulk of her quivered as she tried to hold it in.

Spike was astonished. Amy was amazed, but had the sense to keep silent.

A long moment passed before Mrs. Lowell sobered, took a deep breath, and narrowed her eyes sternly. "I do not approve of what you did, you understand that, don't you?"

"Yes, ma'am," Spike answered quickly. "You bet."

"But you were aiming for your father, right?"

Amy nodded, not daring to speak.

"And you couldn't help it if, from above, Sergeant Silver in civilian clothes looked like him?"

"That's exactly what happened," Spike agreed, and grunted when Amy jabbed an elbow into his side.

Mrs. Lowell rubbed a hand over her face, then back through her hair. "All right." She glanced at the house, lost in thought for a second. "Spike, I have some groceries in the backseat. Take them inside, please."

He nearly flew to the car.

"Amy, my feet are killing me, your father's working late again, and since it's already six o'clock, you're making dinner tonight."

Amy didn't protest. She hated to cook. She would rather eat cold soup from a can. But this was a miracle, and she wasn't about to blow it. She only hoped Spike wouldn't do something stupid. Like—

With two large brown bags scooped into his arms, Spike paused in front of her mother and said, "Mrs. Lowell, it would give me great pleasure if you would permit me to escort your lovely daughter to the cinema this lovely evening."

—that.

Amy groaned silently.

Mrs. Lowell looked at him. "The house needs painting."

He blinked stupidly. "But it's brick!"

"Inside," she ordered. "Before the ice cream melts."

"Right." He backed away. "Yes, ma'am." He turned and practically flew up the steps. "Anything you say."

Once he had fumbled his way inside, Amy waited for her mother to join her. This wasn't natural, and she couldn't understand why the sudden change of heart. Ordinarily, she would already be exiled to her room, no TV, no stereo, and worse—no telephone. On a Saturday night, that meant she might as well have been walled up in a cave.

As they climbed the steps, Mrs. Lowell touched her arm. "The law is to be respected, young lady. I know you know that. And I know it was just a mistake."

"It was, Mom, honest."

Mrs. Lowell opened the door. "But as long as you had to make a mistake, you couldn't have picked a better target."

Amy couldn't move.

Sergeant Silver? A better target?

Don't push it, she cautioned herself; don't get stupid and ask stupid questions. You'll find out soon enough.

The she heard glass shattering and raced into the kitchen. She was just in time to see her mother glaring at Spike, who, in turn, was staring mournfully at a broken jar on the floor. There was tomato sauce everywhere, including his shoes and shins.

He couldn't speak; he could only shake his head.

Mrs. Lowell dropped her pocketbook on the counter and fished inside until she pulled out her wallet. "Clean it up," was all she said, nodding wearily toward the sink and a roll of paper towels. She turned to her daughter and handed her some bills. "When he's done, take this boy out of here before he pulls the house down. Be sure you eat something. Have a good time at the movies. And," she added, raising her voice before Amy could say a word, "if you're not home by eleven . . ."

She didn't have to finish.

A good mood could be stretched only so far.

So Amy gladly helped with the cleanup, put the groceries away, then grabbed Spike's arm and hustled him outside. They considered heading down toward the boardwalk to have something at one of the Surf Road eateries, but decided it was too far to walk. So they ate, as usual, at Red's, a luncheonette across the Row from the theater. Amy liked it because not only was it the off-season hangout for her and her friends, but it was also the only place in town that didn't serve seafood. She hated fish, and nearly everything else that came out of the sea. Burgers or chicken fingers, fries and diet soda—that's all she needed.

Not even the truly awful science fiction film they saw could dampen her mood. Afterward, they stood under the marquee and watched customers lining up for the second show. And when Spike insisted that he walk her home because her mother would kill him if he didn't—and because she needed protection from the Venusian slime monsters lurking in the trees—she grabbed his hand impulsively, yanked him down, and kissed his cheek.

"Hey!" he said, leaning away. "What was that for?"

She didn't know.

It was as much a surprise to her as it was to him.

Before she could come up with a decent answer, however, Becky raced up to them, out of breath.

"Hey, Becky," Spike said. "The movie scared you that much?"

"Jon," Becky answered, gasping for air.

"Jon scared you?"

Becky ignored him. "Amy, Jon's gone."

"What?"

The girl jabbed a thumb over her shoulder. "The houses."

"You're kidding."

She nodded. "He said that if we wouldn't go with him, he'd go by himself."

Amy didn't know what to do. If she went over there and her mother found out, all that good feeling would be just a memory. On the other hand, more than one kid had broken a bone prowling around those decrepit buildings, and she suspected Jon wouldn't be satisfied with simply walking around the outside.

She checked her watch: two hours to eleven.

"Amy," Spike warned.

It wasn't that far. She could get over there, make him change his mind, and be back in plenty of time to avoid her mother's wrath.

Besides, she had a bad feeling about this.

A very bad feeling.

3

No one lived on Storm Hill anymore.

Its seaward face was jagged brown rock in a sheer drop to the water that thundered constantly against it; the southern slope bulged into the Point like a tall and frozen lava flow. It was steep here as well, more stony ground and boulders than trees and underbrush, and more than one developer had been frustrated trying to figure out how to make it less forbidding, more attractive. And the woodland on top had long since reclaimed all attempts to build there.

Maitland Road, like those streets east and west of it, came to a dead end at the hill's base. Most of the houses were small and neatly kept, showing the effects of salt air and weather in a way that made them seem comfortable and solid.

At the north end of the street were three massive and

long-deserted Victorian houses, two crouched on the east side, one on the west. Undeveloped wooded lots separated them from the rest of the block.

Standing in the middle of the blacktop made Amy feel as if she had been thrust backward into the last century. The nearest streetlamp was weak, casting slow, shifting shadows where none should have been. There was a moon, but it only served to make the old houses darker and larger, their gables like blind eyes staring toward the ocean, their wraparound porches cluttered with dark things that moved against the direction of the night wind. Weeds and high grass choked the yards. The solitary house she faced had a fence with more ragged gaps than pickets, and a FOR SALE sign alongside the crumbling stone walk was tilted nearly on its side.

The block was silent.

The voice of the receding tide grumbled at her back.

She wouldn't have been surprised to hear a horse clopping toward her out of the dark, or see an elegant carriage drift into the light.

Becky stood beside her, Spike just behind, nervously jingling his change until Becky snapped at him to knock it off. They peered into the gloom, trying to see which one of the houses Jon had decided to explore.

"He must have brought a flashlight," Spike whispered.

Amy agreed. Even Jon wasn't dumb enough to try this without some light.

She was beginning to wonder why he had seemed so attractive.

Finally Becky touched their arms and suggested they start with the pair on the other side. The yards were less like jungles, and the houses themselves seemed lifeless, so it would make sense that he would give them a try first.

Amy didn't argue. She didn't like it here, and all she wanted now was to find her friend and get home.

They had stopped by Spike's house on the way over, where he had taken two small flashlights from the garage. One he kept for himself, the other he handed to Amy, and the trio moved cautiously to the first building, stepping through a gateless fence and onto the uneven lawn. He warned them as they made their way around the side to keep their lights aimed at the ground as much as they could. It would keep them from tripping over something hidden in the high grass, and it would prevent nosy neighbors from calling the police.

"How do you know so much?" Becky asked quietly.

He shrugged and said nothing.

By the time they had made a complete circuit of the building, it was clear Jon hadn't been there. All the doors and windows were boarded up tightly, and the grass, damp with early dew, hadn't been trampled.

The second house was the same, although they discovered part of an old carriage wheel half-buried beneath a tree in back, and four rusted bedsprings propped against the side of a two-car garage whose roof had partially collapsed. Here, too, the windows were boarded up, and their shutters nailed tightly closed. Shards of broken glass glittered in the weeds, caught by the dim moonlight.

There was no sign of forced entry.

If anyone was actually in there, it would have to be a ghost.

They had just reached the sidewalk again when Spike suddenly rapped her arm with his flashlight and pointed over her shoulder.

A dim light flared in the side yard across the way.

Almost as soon as she spotted it, it was gone.

Becky muttered something under her breath.

Amy looked down the street to be sure no one was watching, then hurried over, through the gate and around to the place where she had seen the glow.

No one was there.

She hissed, trying to get Jon's attention, but the only thing she heard was the strengthening night wind rasping to itself in the trees, and the dry scratch of dead leaves scuttling along the sidewalk.

Cautiously she led the way toward the back, stepping around a pile of debris she couldn't identify. Then she nearly stumbled over a line of large stones that, when she flashed her beam over them, seemed once to have been the border of a garden that was now nothing more than a graveyard for brittle weeds.

A quick sweep of Spike's light showed her the boarded windows, a shutter hanging from one hinge, and a length of clapboard blackened as if by fire. Ribbons of paint hung crookedly from the walls, and there were large gaps where the wind had scoured the wood clean.

She heard the rattle of pebbles bouncing down the slope.

She snapped her head around and stared into the black wall Storm Hill made on her right.

Something had moved up there.

Becky must have heard it too, because she pressed closer, and Amy could hear her nervous breathing.

Spike leaned between them and whispered, "Raccoon, probably. No big deal."

Amy nodded, but she really wasn't convinced. The longer she stayed here, the more she understood why kids didn't use these places as targets for rock-throwing or sites for exploring. There was something about them, and especially about this one, that wouldn't take much to make her believe in ghosts and vampires.

They moved forward again when the faint noise ceased. Suddenly Amy held up her hand.

They heard a muffled footstep behind them, and the crackling of brittle stems.

Jon, she thought, if that's you, I'm going to break your stupid neck.

She aimed the light into the yard, and Jon threw up one arm to shield his eyes from the glare.

"What the . . . ?"

She came very close to laughing aloud as she hurried toward him. He had dressed all in black, and even wore a black ski cap over his hair. She was a little disappointed he hadn't smeared shoe polish or burnt cork over his face too; it would have made the outfit perfect.

He smiled when he recognized them. "Hey, you changed your minds!"

"Not on a bet," Spike answered sourly.

"We came to get you," Becky told him, her voice trembling with relief and anger.

He shook his head. "No way, guys." He pointed at the back porch. "The door's unlocked, man. All I have to do is walk in."

"So why didn't you?" Amy asked. Was he so dense that he couldn't tell how concerned they were?

"Heard a noise."

Becky backed off. "In there?"

"No, dope. It was you, okay? I thought it might be the cops or something."

Spike reached for his arm. "Well, it's not, it's us, and let's disappear before the cops do come and we end up spending the night behind bars, drinking from a tin cup, begging to see the warden."

"That ain't funny, Amanti," Jon snapped, yanking his arm away. "If you're not going to help, why don't you just beat it, okay?"

Amy frowned at the abrupt display of temper; she didn't understand. Earlier, he had behaved as if this was a goof, nothing more. Something to kill a Saturday night with. Something to brag about in school on Monday morning. Now he was sullen, close to anger, and she didn't think it was because they had come to stop him.

She stood to one side with Becky while the two boys argued, neither one giving an inch.

Suddenly she whirled and looked at the house.

She had it.

Becky looked at her. *What?* her expression said.

Amy waved her off and walked over to the boys, gently but firmly pushing Spike aside.

"It's because of Dev, isn't it," she said without giving Jon a chance to protest.

He stared at her, scowling. "You don't know what you're talking about."

"Dev and his brother used to hang around here, right? They live just a couple of blocks up the street."

He looked away.

"This is the place Dev keeps talking about, isn't it," she said quietly, although what she really wanted to do was grab his shoulders and shake some sense into him. "I forget what he calls it. . . . The Forever House, something like that."

Spike snapped his fingers. "Yeah. Right."

"Shut up," Jon snarled. "You're blowing hot air."

Becky planted herself in front of him, forcing him to look at her. "Jon, come on, okay? I mean, I know Dev's our friend and all, but don't you think he's already searched this place a hundred times?"

Jon's chest rose and fell rapidly; his foot tapped the ground angrily. "You don't understand," he finally said.

"I know that coming here in the middle of the night is about as dumb as you can get."

Amy held her breath. She thought Jon was going to

hit her, but Becky stood her ground, matching him glare for glare, until the dangerous moment passed, and he only pushed her away roughly and started for the porch.

"Don't," Amy said.

He didn't stop.

"Jon, please, this is crazy."

Spike ran up to him, grabbed his elbow, and spun him around. "She's right, man, don't. Wait until tomorrow. We'll all go in with you." He jabbed his chin at the house. "You'll kill yourself in there now."

Jon put the flat of his hand against Spike's chest and shoved him so hard, Spike lost his balance and fell onto his back. "Stay away from me," he ordered tautly, his lips barely moving. "Just . . . stay away."

Amy couldn't move.

Not even when she heard Becky crying softly.

With the pale-white beam ahead of him, Jon climbed the steps warily, testing his footing before putting his whole weight down. He did the same as he crossed to the door, reached out, and took hold of the knob.

Then he turned, and Amy saw the grin, the old Jon's grin as he waggled his eyebrows.

"Wish me luck."

"Yeah, sure," Spike said sourly. "Just don't expect me to come running in there after you when you need rescuing."

Jon laughed. "Fat chance."

He pushed the door inward.

The hinges didn't make a sound.

"Kitchen," he called over his shoulder. "Ugly. God, it's ugly."

Becky stalked away then.

Jon stepped up to the threshold, poked his head inside, and looked back at the others. "Last chance, guys." When nobody moved, he clucked like a chicken, and grinned again. "You going to hang around or what?"

Amy almost nodded, then caught herself and just stood there.

"Your loss. I'll tell you all about it tomorrow."

He stepped inside.

She heard him say, "Wow, what a mess," before the door closed softly behind him.

Then there was nothing but the night wind.

Nothing at all.

4

When Jon vanished into the building, Amy's first impulse was to race up the porch, charge inside, grab him by the hair, and drag him back out. Even if he did have a flashlight, and even if he was careful, there was no telling what might have gone wrong in there after all those years of neglect. The floor could be ready to collapse. A ceiling fixture could come down on his head. God knows what kinds of animals were living in there now—rats in the basement, maybe, or rabid bats in the attic.

She shuddered, took a step forward, and stopped herself with a sharp shake of her head.

Spike watched her carefully.

"He'll kill me, won't he?" she said, nodding toward the house.

"He'll kill both of us," he answered. "Because if you're going in, you're sure not going in alone."

She grinned. "You think I can't handle it?"

"Not him, no."

He wasn't smiling.

But he was right.

After what had happened with Becky and Spike earlier, there was no telling what he might do if she—a girl, for crying out loud—tried to bring him out.

Spike gestured her to follow as he made his way around the side of the house. Becky was nowhere to be seen. "Look," he said when she joined him, "there's no sense hanging around, waiting. He'll come out when he comes out, and if we're still here, he's going to blow his top."

"I'd want you to be out here," she said, glancing at the house and shuddering.

"You're not Jon." He swept his beam quickly over the house. "Besides, if he knows we're here, he'll probably stay inside just to make us crazy."

She nodded in agreement. More than just trying to help out a friend, this had evidently become what she and Becky called a "guy thing." It had something to do with pride, a lot to do with stubbornness, and the rest she figured she'd never understand if she lived to be a hundred.

Still, when the wind banged a loose shutter against the wall and the hollow *thump* echoed, she wished he hadn't gone in there alone.

"Anyway," Spike added with a hint of laughter, "if

you hang around much longer, your mother'll have a cow."

With a silent gasp, she brought her watch close to her eyes and realized that she had less than fifteen minutes to get home before eleven.

"I'm outta here," she said, and broke into a trot. Suddenly she turned and added, "Watch out for Becky, okay?"

He nodded as she turned again and sprinted down the walk to the sidewalk, swung right and ran full out. She didn't see Becky at all, didn't hear if Spike was following. All she could think of was Jon messing around in that stupid house, and her mother standing in the doorway, tapping her foot, pointedly staring at her watch. Her father would be in the living room, watching the late news. It wasn't that he didn't care, but when her mother got into one of her moods, he knew better than to try to smooth things over.

Turning the corner at full speed nearly took her into the street, and she slowed a little. A stitch pulled sharply in her side. A dog, invisible on a darkened porch, sounded an alarm as she passed, and she gave it a mocking salute before concentrating on not tripping over shadows.

The chill she had felt on Maitland Road turned to an uncomfortable warmth unusual for late September. Though the night was still cool, she felt as if she had somehow stumbled into a sauna. Her T-shirt clung damply to her chest and back, her jeans felt as if she'd been swimming in them, and the sound of her sneakers

on the pavement reminded her of the sound the palm
of a hand makes as it slaps the water.

She slowed again, one hand gripping her waist until
the stitch subsided. Then she was racing once more,
swinging up the walk, and slamming through the door
just as the hall clock chimed the eleventh hour.

Her mother looked up from the couch. "You shouldn't
run like that, dear," she said calmly. "You'll overexert
yourself."

Her father raised an eyebrow, but didn't ask. Instead, he wanted to know if the movie was as bad as he
had heard it was. When she told him he'd heard right,
he only grunted and said, "The world ain't the same
since John Wayne died."

She laughed, blew them both kisses, bade them
goodnight, and trudged up to her room. After stripping
and drying herself off, she flopped onto her bed, pulled
up the sheet and thin blanket, and stared at the
crosshatch shadow of a windowpane on the ceiling.

She heard the clock strike eleven-thirty.

He'll be finished by now, she figured. She hoped.

When the clock chimed midnight, she felt the first
twinge of guilt at leaving him alone. Before she could
think about it, however, she fell asleep.

And awoke in a room painted completely white.

There were no windows, no doors, nothing to sit on,
nothing on the walls.

She could hear a regular, dull thudding, the sound of
her heart beating.

And a small distant voice that said, *Amy, help me, I'm lost.*

And awoke in a room painted completely red.

There were no windows, no doors, nothing to sit on, nothing on the walls but a large spiderweb in the far corner that trembled in a breeze she could neither feel nor hear.

The dried husk of a moth hung in the center.

The twisted husk of a fly lay on the floor.

The spider was gone.

There was nothing but a distant voice that begged, *Amy, help me, I'm lost.*

And awoke in a room painted completely black.

There were no windows, no doors, nothing to sit on, nothing on the walls but a large, gold-framed mirror covered with brown dust.

There was no sound at all, not even her heart.

She walked over to the mirror and tried to see her face. When she failed, she dried her hand on her leg and wiped a clear spot in the middle of the glass.

What she saw wasn't her reflection.

It was Jon.

He stood in a room painted white, and red, and black.

He was screaming.

She awoke in a room painted in soft blues and gentle white, a dresser against the far wall next to a vanity, cluttered bookshelves over an unfinished pine desk. Posters of rock stars and movies took up most of the walls, and on the floor there was wall-to-wall carpeting, here and there strewn with clothes not yet put away.

The room was stifling and sweat trickled down her cheeks, but she felt winter-cold.

Her mouth opened to cry out until she realized where she was. Dreams, she told herself; you're okay, they were only dreams.

The hall clock struck two.

With one hand to her chest to steady her breathing, she sat up and switched on the nightstand light, just to be sure, then switched it off again and sagged back onto her pillow, sheet and blanket clutched loosely to her throat. While she slept, someone had drawn the curtains over her window, and the shadow of the pane was gone from the ceiling.

Her girlfriends had told her of having dreams about boys, and she had had them herself a number of times. But nightmares? This was a new one, and she didn't like it at all. Tomorrow she'd call Jon's house and ream him out good for being such a jerk, for making her lose sleep just because he wanted to be big and brave and stupid.

The memory of the nightmares shredded like clouds in the wind.

Or maybe she wouldn't call. Maybe she would let him call her to apologize.

She shivered, felt a sneeze threaten to explode and fade before she could grab for a tissue.

Then she closed her eyes and counted to ten.

When she opened them again, sunlight had brightened the tufted white curtains. She tried to sit up, groaned, and fell back. "No," she whispered. "Oh, no." Her head felt as if it had been stuffed with wet cotton, and what seemed like every bone from neck to knee ached. Sighing, she curled onto her side as a cough tore her throat. Great, she thought, and coughed again.

Just . . . great.

She lay dozing for another hour before stumbling into the bathroom. Her reflection looked awful. Her hair was stuck damply to her forehead, red-rimmed eyes stared blearily back at her, and a faint flush made her cheeks shine.

Great.

Making her way down to the kitchen was a chore; listening to her mother fuss over her was worse. But she was in no shape to argue. All she wanted to do was crawl back into bed and forget the world existed. And after forcing down some raisin toast and orange juice, she did just that, not waking again until the sun had set.

Her head was a little better, but her cough hadn't improved. And when her telephone rang, she almost didn't answer.

"Hey, Net," Spike said.

She grunted; it was the best she could do. As it was, she wheezed every time she took a breath.

"Boy, you sound awful."

"Thanks. I feel lousy."

He sneezed, coughed, and cleared his throat noisily. "Me, too."

She slumped on the mattress, the receiver pinned beneath her ear. "You talk to Jon today?"

"Tried a couple of times, but no one answered. I've been lying on the couch catching a game. I don't feel like doing anything else." Another cough, this one long and harsh. "I think I'd better go now."

"Wait! Aren't you even going to apologize?"

"For what?"

"Giving me this cold, flu, whatever it is."

He sneezed. "Ask me again tomorrow if I'm still alive."

He hung up.

She dropped the receiver back onto its cradle and tried to think if she had any homework for tomorrow. She might have; she couldn't remember. Not that it made any difference. She wasn't in any shape to do much more than just lie here anyway.

Time dragged.

Her parents checked on her now and then, fed her juice and aspirin, whispering as though they were in a hospital room. When she insisted she was all right, that all she needed was rest, they nodded maddeningly, mopped her brow, and tiptoed out.

Some of the kids, she knew, didn't mind getting sick once in a while. It got them out of school, and got their folks to wait on them.

She hated it.

It annoyed her to be treated like a baby, despite all the aches and pains; but most of all, she hated the helplessness, the weakness, as if, somehow, it was all her fault.

Shortly after eleven, her parents went to bed.

Shortly after midnight, she drifted into a fitful sleep.

And saw the red room.

The white room.

The black room with its mirror.

But she didn't see Jon, and she didn't hear him at all.

When she woke the next morning, the cough was gone and she felt only slightly groggy. It took a few minutes, but she convinced her mother that she was well enough to go to school; but only after she promised—cross her heart—that one sneeze or cough would bring her home again.

"You're not Supergirl, you know," her mother said.

Amy sniffed and blew her nose. "Tell me about it."

Luckily the sun was out, the day comfortably warm, and the only hint of coming autumn were a few maple trees already sporting spots of gold. The fresh air made her feel much better, and when she reached Tidal Row even her head had cleared.

As she waited for the traffic light to change, someone called her name.

It was Becky, whose face held all the evidence of her own bout with Spike's cold. They exchanged sympathies, and vows to get even, before Becky said, "Have you heard from Jon?"

5

Beachland High School was on a block all its own. It was a large brick-and-marble building three stories high, its windows tall and arched, its main entrance flanked by massive marble columns. Evergreen shrubs grew high and thick along its foundation, a narrow lawn ran across its front, and a flagpole grew from an island of flowers in the middle of the wide, concrete walk that led to the front steps.

Amy stood by the pole, searching the crowd for Jon or Spike, but it was hopeless. On a day like this, everybody was waiting until the last possible second before going inside, and when the warning bell rang and the surge began toward the doors, it was all she could do to keep from being carried along. There were only a dozen or so seniors left, lounging on the grass,

before she gave up and went in, ducking into home-
room just as the last bell sounded.

Then the boy who sat behind her asked someone
else for cheat notes for the biology test, and she nearly
shrieked aloud. She had forgotten all about it, and
spent the rest of the day grabbing every second to go
over her notes, skim the thick textbook, and pray that
Mrs. Samson wasn't going to be too hard on them so
early in the year.

Mrs. Samson, however, seemed to think that early
or late, her classes weren't going to be given a single
break. Amy nearly wept when she saw the first
question.

By the time the release bell rang, she was a nervous
wreck. She knew she hadn't failed, but she also knew
that this wasn't going to be one of her better grades.
Plus, she hadn't seen anyone all day. Spike had
apparently gone home early, Becky just wasn't anywhere she usually was, and Jon, for all she could tell,
hadn't even bothered to show up.

She left the school in a daze, that stuffy feeling
creeping over her again. It wasn't until she reached the
sidewalk that she realized someone was following her,
trying to get her attention without using her name.

She turned, and Dev Costello nearly collided with
her.

There was a flurry of awkward apologies, a frantic
grab for her books sliding out of her grip, and a sudden
silence as they faced each other, not knowing what to
say.

Amy sneezed.

"Bless you," the boy said automatically.

"Thanks. So, what's up?"

Dev was tall and lanky, his hair much like Becky's—long, straight, and white-blond. He was a sophomore, and a substitute on the JV basketball team, but somehow she didn't think playing the game was his idea. He was also incredibly, painfully shy. He probably hadn't said more than two words to her at a time in all the years she'd known him.

"Jon," he finally said, looking everywhere but at her.

"What about him?"

He shrugged with one bony shoulder. "I've, uh, been kind of looking for him, I guess." Another shrug. "You, uh, know where he is?"

"I haven't seen him all day, Dev."

"Okay."

But he didn't move.

When she couldn't stand the silence anymore, she began to sidle away, smiling inanely. He was a nice guy and all, but he was giving her the creeps. "Well, look, if I see him, I'll tell him you're looking for him." She made a point of showing him her watch. "Got to run. Homework, you know?" She turned her back to cross the street, looked over her shoulder and added, "Take it easy. See you."

She had one foot on the street when she heard him say, "Forever House."

She stopped and turned slowly. "What?"

The boy still wouldn't look at her. "I think . . . I think he went into the Forever House."

Amy wasn't sure what to do. He seemed upset, and probably wouldn't want to hear that that's exactly where Jon had gone. On the other hand, curiosity about what he'd called that old place couldn't be denied.

"You know," she said at last, "I think you and I have to talk."

He blushed.

She couldn't believe it. He actually blushed, and it almost made her laugh.

"It's okay," she told him, taking his arm. "We won't go to Red's or anything. Let's go around to the bleachers, okay? It'll be quiet there, pretty much."

His face grew redder, but he didn't pull away, and they walked around the building to the playing fields in back. The cross country team ran laps on the dark cinder track; the girls' field hockey team had a game on their field near the back fence; and only a handful of kids sat in the high wood bleachers, most of them girls waiting for their boyfriends.

Amy climbed straight to the top row, Dev reluctantly following. When she picked a place to sit, she couldn't help noticing that his spot was to her left and a row down, well out of her reach. As if, she thought, confused, he was really afraid of her.

If it hadn't been for the dismal look on his face, she probably would have teased him about it. As it was, she forced herself to wait until he spoke first.

"My brother went in there, you know," he said at last. He stared at the kids scattered across the grass and track, but she knew he wasn't seeing a thing. "He went in there. He never came out."

They called it the Forever House, he said, because that's what it looked like—as if it had been there forever. They had never been inside, but they liked to explore the yard and the hillside when they were little. When Matt became a senior, he seemed to forget about the place, and Dev was too interested in other things.

Then, a week before graduation, his brother told him he was going to give himself a special present for getting out of Beachland in one piece. He was finally going to do a little exploring.

Dev thought he was being a jerk.

Matt said it was just a game, don't worry about it.

Two days after the ceremony, Matt told him the time had come. The parties were over, summer had begun, and because the next day he had to start work on the boardwalk, he was going to spend his last free night sneaking around the Forever House, checking it out.

Dev didn't much care one way or the other. He still thought it was dumb, but his big brother always did what he wanted anyway, no matter what anyone said.

The following morning, Matt hadn't returned.

Dev said nothing to his parents, but snuck off to Maitland Road and had a look around. He saw nothing that indicated Matt had even been there, and when he went inside the house, there was enough dust on the kitchen floor to show him that only small animals had ever been in there.

The rest of the house was the same.

At least on the ground floor. He never went upstairs, or down in the cellar. He didn't have to.

Matt wasn't there, and never had been.

Like everyone else, he had come to believe that his brother had left town without telling a soul.

The problem was, he didn't know why.

Matt didn't fight with his brother or parents any more than anyone else did. He had a hundred girls dying to go out with him, and was planning on joining the Army at summer's end, to take advantage of the college plan . . . and to get away from Taggard Point.

"I guess I could live with that," he said. "But then the dreams started."

Amy had let him go on without interruption. She hadn't a clue why he was telling her all of this. They weren't friends, not really, and moved in different circles at school and away. But he was clearly agitated about Jon, and probably figured he and Amy were going together.

Still, none of it made much sense until he mentioned the dreams.

She clasped her knees tightly and hoped her voice wouldn't shake. "What . . . what dreams?"

He told her.

Her eyes closed, opened, and she whispered, "What did you see?"

He told her.

Her stomach lurched.

She had never believed in dreams being omens, or

signs pointing to the future. The supernatural existed only in books and movies, and late at night on someone's porch when she and friends tried to scare each other.

And this, of course, could simply be coincidence. Things like that happened all the time. There was nothing weird about that, nothing out of the ordinary, not really.

She had to ask: "Did you . . . in the dreams, did you hear anything?"

He told her.

Oh my God, she thought. Oh my God.

He twisted around to look up at her for the first time. "You think I'm crazy."

She denied it instantly, but he shook his head with a sad smile.

"It's okay, you don't have to lie. No one else believes me either. They think I'm nuts or something, too." The smile vanished; his face became hard, much older. "If Jon went in there, Amy, you've got to do something to get him out. I don't know . . . I don't know what's going on, but . . ." Suddenly he grabbed his books and stood.

A small cloud edged in black drifted under the sun.

"The dreams stopped a long time ago," he said. "I think my brother's . . ." He swallowed, looked away, and chopped the air with his free hand. "Forget it. It's crazy." He chopped the air again, helplessly, and said nothing more. He sidled into the aisle and started down.

"Dev, wait!"

He didn't stop. He moved more quickly instead, and by the time Amy had snatched up her own books, he was at the bottom and running.

"Dev!"

He was gone.

She followed slowly, agreeing that it was totally crazy, that there was a place someone could walk into and disappear like that. Assuming that Matt had even gone there in the first place. Nobody had seen him, and Dev admitted that he himself had searched the house pretty thoroughly and had found nothing—why would he think his brother was still there?

The dreams.

She shivered.

The same dreams, the same voice.

Help me, Amy, I'm lost.

6

She was too upset to go home right away.

She wandered aimlessly for a while before finding herself on Surf Road, the broad avenue that ran between the town and the boardwalk, which itself ended on the north where Storm Hill reared out of the sea, and at Embankment Park, where the narrow Indian River had its mouth.

Sea gulls floated effortlessly on the breeze, searching for handouts, as she crossed over to the boardwalk. A dozen terns raced each other along the beach's wet apron, searching for sand crabs. All the buildings that faced the Atlantic on the other side of the street had once been houses; now they were mostly shops and restaurants, arcades and keno parlors, bed-and-breakfast establishments and tiny hotels. The only construction on the boardwalk itself was on WonderLand Pier, two blocks down, and Shipport Pier, three blocks north.

She walked toward Storm Hill.

Despite the lovely day, she was alone, and she preferred it that way. The ocean's constant thunder was comforting in many ways, the hypnotic rush and retreat of the waves allowing her to remove all distractions when she had to have time to think.

When she had walked a couple of blocks, she drifted to the boardwalk's edge. A green, three-rail metal fence separated her from a six-foot drop to the sand, and she dropped her books, slipped her legs under the bottom rail, and folded her arms on the middle one.

She stared at the water.

Crazy, she thought; this is crazy.

If it hadn't been for those awful nightmares, she would have dismissed Dev's story out of hand. He missed his brother, that was obvious. Since he couldn't bring himself to believe that Matt had really run away—if eighteen-year-olds can run away—he had had to come up with another explanation.

And, she realized, resting her chin on a forearm, he hadn't mentioned a third, distasteful possibility—that something had happened to Matt.

Something fatal.

She vaguely remembered the police searching Storm Hill and the pine forest on the other side at the time. There was, she also recalled, a search of the river. "Covering all bases," her father had called it, although he also told her mother he didn't think it was necessary. The boy had simply taken off, and would no doubt resurface when he was good and ready.

Maybe her father had been wrong.

All right, she asked herself, then explain the dreams.

She couldn't.

A black-masked gull settled on the sand below her to pick at a scattering of broken shells.

"What do you think?" she asked it.

Startled, it cried out and flew away.

She grinned. "Right. It's dumb."

Slowly she turned her head, gazing up the length of the beach. Four boys played catch on the sand near the amusement pier, a dog racing among them, its tail wagging furiously. An elderly couple bundled up as if for winter settled on one of the wooden benches that faced the ocean. When she lifted her gaze, she spotted the skeleton of the Ferris wheel at the end of Wonder-Land, its cages gone.

And there, strolling up the boards toward her, was Spike Amanti, in sweatpants and sweatshirt, its floppy hood pulled over his head. He coughed into a fist and broke into a slow trot, his arms loose at his sides.

He sat beside her, arms propped on the middle rail, hands dangling.

"How was school?"

She grunted. "Biology test."

"Nuts," he said. "Forgot all about it."

She grinned without looking at him. "I'll bet."

"I have a terrible cold, I want you to know."

"You don't have to tell me that. You gave it to me and Becky."

"Becky, too?"

She nodded.

"Sorry."

They watched the waves, the ballplayers, and followed a pair of gulls sweeping low over the water. The silhouette of a large ship crawled along the horizon.

"I had a dream last night," he said, and poked his head through the rails to stare down at the sand. "I lie. It wasn't a dream, it was a nightmare."

She told him Dev's story, and he said, "I don't want to hear it."

A few seconds later: "Maybe it's . . . forget it."

A few seconds after that: "We're in the *Twilight Zone*, you know. It isn't real. It's just TV."

He pushed his hood back. "In *my* dream he said, 'Help me, Spike, I'm lost'."

Without speaking, they climbed back to their feet, Spike took her books, and they hurried to the first public phone booth they could find, on a corner near a neon-outlined bar. Two attempts to get ahold of Becky failed. They headed away from the beach, not sure where they were going until they found themselves crossing Maitland Road. They exchanged unreadable glances before turning onto the street.

In daylight it looked no different than any other street in the Point. Some of the houses were old, some were new, most were solidly in between. The trees were high and full, many of them slightly bent away from the nearly constant onshore breeze. Little kids played in yards, pets prowled, cars were parked in driveways.

It was so normal, she began to think she had imagined the whole thing.

Until they reached the last block.

Sunlight filtered gold through the leaves. A large crow strutted across the blacktop. Rising above it all, Storm Hill looked perfectly ordinary. Yet as she walked, Amy couldn't help but imagine that the light was somehow different around the Forever House. Dimmer. Flecked with motes of dust. As if the ancient building had been shrouded in a pale, gray veil that rippled in the breeze.

"It looks," Spike said, "as if a good wind would blow it down."

He was right. The peeling paint, hanging shutters, sagging porch roof, and a ragged gap in the steps made it appear as if only habit were holding it up. All it needed was one good kick, and it would crumple into dust.

It didn't look frightening at all.

It just looked sad.

They angled toward the fence, trying to look as if they were only out for an innocent walk, which, Amy realized, was pretty hard to do with the hill in the way and no place else to go but back. She picked up a long piece of dead branch and slapped it against the pickets. The noise sounded like gunshots.

Spike tucked his hands into his sweatshirt pockets and walked blithely into the front yard, studying the old house intently. He stepped back. He moved closer. He shifted toward the side yard and peered up at the peaked roof.

Puzzled, Amy followed him, mimicking his feigned interest until they were out of sight of the rest of the neighborhood. Then they headed straight for the back, where they found Becky sitting on the ground, staring at the back door. Her gaze shifted when they walked up, but she didn't move.

All she said was, "He's still in there."

That's when Amy finally realized that Becky had fallen in love. It was, now that she thought about it, so obvious she must have been blind not to notice it before. All this time trying to get Jon hooked up with her, and Becky had fallen prey to her own tricks.

Amy knelt beside her. "I want to ask you a question."

Becky nodded.

"It's going to sound dumb."

Becky looked at her, her face drawn and pale.

"Last night . . ." She cleared her throat. "Did you . . . did you have any dreams?"

The girl didn't have to answer; Amy saw it in her eyes.

"So now what?" Spike asked.

"I suggest," a voice answered, "you begin with an explanation."

They jumped to their feet, startled, as Sergeant

Silver stepped into the open. His gray-and-gold uniform was snug and starched, his black boots gleaming in the late-afternoon sun. He stiffened when he recognized the trio, and Amy knew immediately nothing they could say would satisfy him. Evidently one of the neighbors had seen them, and naturally, teenagers around a crumbling house could only mean trouble.

"Well?" the policeman demanded.

"Just looking," Spike answered, kicking at the ground.

"Just looking," the man repeated flatly. He scanned the house and the yard. "You wouldn't be thinking about going in there, would you?"

"Gosh, no," Spike said. He looked at the others for corroboration. "No way. Never." The girls shook their heads as well.

"Gosh," the officer echoed. Flatly. "No way."

Amy didn't know what to do. The policeman's eyes were hidden behind dark glasses, and his thin lips showed no trace of humor. He scanned the area again and stepped to one side.

"Beat it."

They didn't need to be told twice.

Huddled together, they eased around him, but not before he tapped Amy's shoulder with a stiff, hard finger. "I'll be watching you, young lady," he warned. "I don't care who your old man is, I'll be watching you."

A dozen responses, not many of them polite, fought for release, but for a change she managed to find the one that mattered. "Yes, sir."

He nodded.

She hurried to catch up with Spike and Becky, and as soon as they reached the sidewalk, they broke into a run that had them at the corner and across the street in record time. When they slowed to catch their breaths, Silver's cruiser passed. He didn't look in their direction.

"I'm watching you," Spike said, ducking his head and deepening his voice.

Becky giggled.

Amy didn't think it was funny.

"It's the hoosegow for you, young lady."

Becky slapped his arm.

"This town ain't big enough for both of us," he went on.

"Spike . . ." She didn't finish. Instead she pushed between them and grabbed their arms. "We have to go back, you know."

Spike's act crumbled. "Hey, didn't you hear what the man just said?"

All Becky said was, "Jon."

It didn't take long to coordinate their stories. Though it was a school night, they had no doubt they'd be able to get out for a while, as long as their excuse sounded legitimate, and as long as they didn't stay away for too long.

They parted a block later, and Amy quickened her stride, anxious now to get supper over with.

It didn't occur to her to be frightened until she walked breezily into the kitchen just in time to hear her father tell her mother, "I don't know, Vera. God knows he isn't the happiest kid in the world."

"Who?" Amy asked, leaning over the stove to check on the menu.

"Dev Costello."

She didn't move. "What happened?"

"Far as I know, it looks like he's run away."

7

Supper was tasteless, and twice she had to be reprimanded for playing with her food.

Her father had no answers to her hundred questions except to wonder aloud when this boy he didn't even know had suddenly become such a close friend.

"He's not," she insisted, staring glumly at her plate. "I just know him, that's all."

"And that's all *I* know," he told her. "He went to school, he didn't go home, and there were clothes and a backpack missing from his closet, and some money from his dresser. Anything else, you'll have to ask the police."

The subject was closed, she could tell by his tone. And just as she had a hundred questions more, she also wanted to tell him that she was pretty sure she knew where Dev was. But if she said anything, she would have to explain it all—Jon, the shared nightmares, Dev's story—and it didn't require a genius to figure out he wouldn't believe a word.

Nor would the police.

After dessert, when her mother volunteered to take over the dishwashing chores, she made only a token argument before drifting into the living room, then back out again, where her father met her in the foyer.

"Amy, are you all right?"

"Yeah." She shrugged. "I guess so."

He laid the back of his hand against her brow and her cheeks, concern pinching his features. "No coughing, sneezing, anything like that?"

"I'm fine, Dad. Honest."

His expression told her he didn't quite believe her, but she was saved from further questioning when the telephone rang. She ran back into the living room, threw herself on the couch, and snatched up the receiver.

It was Becky, just as they'd planned, casually inviting her over for a cram session in math. When Amy relayed the request in a yell to her father, who was already halfway up to the second floor, he backed down to the bottom step and gave her a mock scowl.

"I am not deaf," he declared.

"Sorry. Can I go?"

"No coughing?"

"No sneezing, no fever, no aches, no nothing."

He gave her a long steady look. "You're amazing, do you know that? Simply amazing."

"What? What did I say?"

He couldn't resist a grin. "It's what you don't say, darlin', that gets me worried sometimes. You were in pretty bad shape yesterday, you know."

"I heal fast," she explained, making it sound as if he should have known it.

"Sure." He took a step up and paused to release a mighty sneeze. "Swell." He looked at her again. "You know what George Bernard Shaw said about the young?"

She rolled her eyes. "Dad, come on."

His hand fluttered in defeat toward the kitchen. "If your mother says okay, then go ahead. But," he added with an upraised finger, "ten o'clock."

She groaned loudly for his benefit, whispered to Becky all was well, reminded her to contact Spike, and hung up.

You're nuts, you know, she told herself.

She agreed. She even agreed that she was probably asking for major trouble.

But she couldn't forget the dreams.

She couldn't forget the fear and sorrow on Dev's face.

"All right, then," she whispered, swinging to her feet. "If you're going to do it, then do it."

She rushed into the kitchen where she teased her mother into giving her the last step of permission, then raced to her bedroom to grab the right book, and a notebook and pen for authenticity. She gave a moment's thought for the sure-to-be-chilly night and an image of the house, and she changed into an old pair of jeans, a shirt, and pullover sweater, and her hanging-around sneakers. She relied on Spike to bring the flashlights again, but during a quick stop in the living room, she slipped a pack of her father's matches into her pocket, just in case.

Fifteen minutes later she was out the door and running for Becky's.

The night was clear, a bite in the air reminding her that autumn wasn't all that far away.

The slap of her footsteps sounded awfully lonely.

Becky was already anxiously pacing the sidewalk a block from her house when Amy arrived, and Spike came running up not two minutes later. They had both heard about Dev, and it was clear their nerves weren't as steady as they had been earlier that afternoon.

This wasn't one of Jon's games anymore; this wasn't one of Amy's elaborate plans.

As they headed for Maitland Road, Amy kept up a constant chatter, earnestly reassuring them it wouldn't take them all that long, especially now that they knew someone else was already in the house. Besides, how long could it take to check a few rooms? With the four of them working rapidly, they could be in and out in less than half an hour. One hour, tops.

Neither asked what they would do if they didn't find Jon.

The walk seemed to take forever.

A police siren cried in the distance, rising and falling before fading into silence.

Spike kept turning around, walking backward, explaining that he was keeping an eye out for Sergeant

Silver. When Becky pointed out that the man's shift must have ended hours ago, Spike reminded her about the warning, saying that he wouldn't put it past the sergeant to take a double shift just to see if he could catch them.

"Paranoid," Becky said.

"I don't like jails," he answered.

"Knock it off," Amy told them. She was apprehensive enough without those two making it worse. Still, she couldn't keep from checking every shadow, every porch, every yard. She was beginning to feel as if she were about to rob a bank, and there was a huge neon arrow following her overhead, flashing on and off as a beacon for the police.

"Tell me again what Dev said," Becky asked her.

Amy did readily, and when she was finished, they were huddled so close together, their shadows on the pavement had merged into one.

They stayed that way until they reached Maitland Road, where Spike stopped them on the corner and checked the streets in all directions. When he was satisfied, he wiped his palms on his jeans, then back through his hair.

"Look, I know how you feel," he said to Amy, "but we really don't have to do this, you know. I mean, it's not too late to forget it."

She just stared at him.

He turned to Becky. "Dev's there now. He'll find Jon, no sweat. Why should we risk getting caught too?"

"The red room," was all Becky said.

He opened his mouth to retort, and closed it again with a loud sigh. "Okay. But if I break a leg, you're carrying me to the hospital."

"Deal," she answered.

"Great," he muttered.

Amy grabbed his hand and squeezed it quickly. "Quit stalling."

"I'm not," he protested, not very convincingly.

She gave his hand another squeeze, and started up the sidewalk, watching her shadow float darkly over the pavement. She wasn't worried about him; he wouldn't let her down. He would complain to the last second, but she knew instinctively he wouldn't let her down. Just as she wasn't about to let Jon down. She had no idea what had caused the three of them to have the same dream, but whether she believed in portents or not, this was something she couldn't ignore.

No matter how much it scared her.

They stood in front the house.

Storm Hill whispered to them.

A slow breeze coasted in from the sea, damp and chilly.

The house had grown dark again, barely seen at the fringe of the streetlamp's reach.

Spike gave them each a flashlight small enough to stick into their hip pockets if they had to. Then he reached under the back of his sweater and pulled out a monkey wrench he tapped against his palm.

"Just in case," he said with a slightly embarrassed shrug. "You never know, right?"

Becky rubbed her upper arms briskly. "Can we just get on with it, please?" Her voice was quiet, but the words shook a little.

Amy knew their nerve, and hers, was about to fail. If any one of the people who lived on this block came out now and demanded to know what they thought they were doing, they'd be gone quicker than lightning.

With a deep breath for courage, then, she strode boldly through the gate and made her way around the side of the house. She didn't look back. She only watched the moonlight turn the ground to silver, and turn the trees a ghostly gray. A small animal scurried through the weeds. A dislodged stone rolled down the side of the hill.

If anyone touches me now, she thought, I'm going to scream bloody murder.

She stumbled over the garden stones, but once in the backyard, she headed directly for the steps, not giving herself a chance to think about what she was doing.

Until she saw the door.

The moon didn't quite reach under the porch roof, yet the door was visible as a black smudge against the night.

Spike came up on her left, Becky on her right.

"In and out," he said. "Right?"

"Absolutely," Becky answered.

Suddenly a phantom of blue and red swirled into the yard, the whine of a large engine not far behind.

"Silver!" Spike said.

There was no time for thought—the trio raced up

the stairs and across the porch, slapped open the door, and ducked inside. Amy turned as she dropped into a crouch and shut the door behind her.

Seconds later the slashing beam of a powerful hand-held light slanted through gaps in the kitchen windows' shutters. Heavy footsteps tramped through the yard. As the fragmented light snapped around the room, she saw high and low cupboards without doors, a large sink darkly stained along its porcelain rim, an electric stove that had to be at least forty years old, and a squat refrigerator that once had been white. The floor was patched linoleum, bare hardwood showing through in more places than not.

Then the footsteps faded and took the light with them.

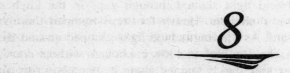

8

Amy lost track of the time as they waited for the cruiser's engine to start. When it did, she held her breath and closed her eyes, praying the policeman wouldn't have second thoughts. Then the engine roared once, subsided, and she heard the vehicle move down the street.

A few seconds later nothing but silence remained.

Still, they waited five minutes more, listening hard to the hush of the soft sea wind outside, and the creaks and barely audible groans of the house as it shifted and settled.

The smell of age and dust, mold and rot made Amy's nose twitch, and she rubbed it furiously, to keep herself from sneezing.

Finally Spike switched on his flashlight, cupping one hand over the face to diffuse the beam so it wouldn't blind them. Amy's vision took a while to adjust to the new twilight inside; once it did, she and Becky turned their own lights on.

"Boy, Jon was right," Spike said quietly. "This place is ugly."

They moved slowly around the room which, Amy estimated, was probably large enough to serve a small army. She had never seen a kitchen so huge, and spotted a quartet of faded circles on the checkerboard linoleum which, she figured, was where a large table once stood. Although she was impatient to get on to the rest of the house, she checked those few cupboards whose doors were still attached, to see if anything had been left behind. Then she froze when Becky tested the faucet, which banged and sputtered without spitting water until she shut it off and wiped her hands on her sweater.

They were stalling again.

Amy didn't mind.

Now that she was here, her bravado had changed to extreme caution.

She had been in old houses before, even a couple that weren't inhabited.

This didn't feel like any of them.

For some odd reason, it didn't feel empty.

The entrance to the rest of the house was a swinging door directly opposite the porch exit. It was propped open, her light told her, by a thick wedge of rubber jammed under the bottom. Beyond was nothing but black; not even a speck of light drifted in from the street.

She approached it with small steps.

Perspiration trickled down her spine, and she felt the stirring of a headache as she unconsciously tried to stare through the gloom.

"Hey," Spike whispered. "Look at this."

On a counter near the door was a shoebox. Inside were at least a dozen more of the solid rubber doorstops.

"Maybe you should take them," Becky suggested.

"What for? They're heavy."

Amy ignored them. She had reached the threshold and found herself at the foot of a long hallway. To her right the wall was marked with four doors; the wall on her left was the paneled base of a staircase, with only one door there—probably the entrance to the basement.

She called Jon's name.

Her voice echoed faintly.

She called to Dev.

There was no response.

Twice more she tried, and failed, to get a response, and the first chilly touch of real fear crawled across the back of her neck.

"Maybe they're hurt or something," Becky suggested at her shoulder.

"I don't know."

Spike tried yelling at the top of his voice.

Only echoes replied.

"This place is bigger than it looks," he said.

"If we split up," Becky said, "we can cover more rooms in less time."

"Oh, right," he said. "Don't you ever go to the movies, Beck? Don't you know what happens when they split up to investigate the haunted house?" He made a cutting noise as he drew a finger across his throat. "No, thank you. This boy ain't going nowhere alone."

"Then let's get to it," Amy said. "We haven't got all night."

They crowded into the hallway, feet shuffling through the unmarked dust. Cobwebs swayed from the high ceiling corners. Bundles of dust lay against the baseboards. The wallpaper was water-stained and streaked with what Amy's imagination screamed was dried blood.

Becky opened the first door and shone her light in. The room was empty.

The basement door was jammed, and Spike swore when he scraped a knuckle trying to force it open.

"Forget it," Amy told him. "If we can't get it open, they probably didn't."

She called out again.

Becky tried as well.

Spike checked the second door and discovered a very small room with a single, ladder-back chair inside. Otherwise, it was empty.

Amy breathed a little easier. No ghosts, no ghouls, no vampires leapt out of the darkness; no aliens from another planet dropped onto them from the ceiling. This place was nothing more than it seemed—an old, dying house.

The third room was the same as the others.

Now, Amy could aim her light up the stairs, through the warped spindles of a banister. Faded rectangles on the wall showed her where pictures had once hung; several pitted brass fixtures marked the spots where gaslights had once burned.

"Boy, this is long," Spike muttered.

Amy glanced behind her. The kitchen, and the exit, seemed a long way off.

The fourth door was actually two doors that slid open under an archway. She gripped the latches and pulled. Nothing happened. She tried again, and winced at the scraping sound they made as they disappeared into the walls.

"Parlor," she announced, peering inside.

Becky called up the stairs for Jon.

Again, the room was empty. A fireplace on the far wall was empty as well. Only a few slants of pale light intruded from the street.

Across the foyer, sliding doors were already open, and she could see what was probably the dining room. A long table sat in the middle of the floor, but there were no chairs.

Street light didn't enter this room at all.

"They're not here," Becky said from the foot of the stairs. Her voice betrayed her; she was ready to cry. "They won't answer."

Spike sneezed, blaming it on the dust.

Knowing what would happen anyway, Amy tried the front door, not surprised when she found it securely locked.

She turned around. "Upstairs, I guess."

Becky flapped her arms helplessly. "But they don't answer, Net."

"It's okay," Spike told her gently. "A place this big, with walls this thick the way they used to build them, you could probably blast your stereo in one room and the guy next door wouldn't hear a thing."

She seemed doubtful, but he didn't give her a chance to think about it. He took her hand, gave a tug, and began to climb the stairs.

Amy's foot was on the bottom step when she thought she heard something.

"Hold it."

They waited.

She checked back the way they had come, aiming the light ahead of her like a spear. The hallway was empty, but she heard it again—a rustling sound, as if something was moving slowly, and deliberately, along the baseboard. Nothing was there, however, and she thought that whatever it was might have gone into the kitchen.

"Don't," Spike warned as she started forward.

"It's okay. Wait there."

She moved on the balls of her feet, right hand trailing along the staircase wall while her left hand kept her light aimed at the far end. It was probably nothing more than a mouse or a rat, but even if it was, the creature had to have come from somewhere; and so far, she hadn't seen as much as a crack large enough to let in a moth.

When she reached the door, she accidentally kicked

the rubber wedge loose, yelped and stumbled back as the door swung closed. Without a sound.

Spike leaned over the banister. "Net, you okay?"

She squinted against the light. "Yeah." She was disgusted with herself. "Just scared myself, that's all. Shine your light over here, okay?"

She reached down and picked up the doorstop, hefting it in her free hand. It was heavier than it looked, and solid; she would hate to have someone hit her with it. A headache would be the least of her troubles.

She shoved the door open, ready to startle whatever she had followed.

Instead, she let the door close.

"Spike?"

It swung easily, and slowly.

"What?"

She couldn't speak.

Footsteps hurried down the stairs, around the newel post and down the hall.

The door kept swinging, the gap smaller with each arc.

Impossible, she thought, catching flashes of the room beyond when the door's opening permitted; it's impossible, I'm just imagining it.

"What's up?" Spike asked.

She pointed. "Open the door."

He laughed. "Hey, you scared of a little mouse?"

She shook her head, reached out, and grabbed Becky's hand. "No. Not a mouse."

"Oh, God," Becky said. "Don't tell me it's a rat. I

hate rats. They carry plague and disease and . . ." She shuddered. "I don't care what it is, just don't let it be a rat."

Spike hesitated, then shoved the door open with his foot, flashlight extended, the monkey wrench held high over his head. Just as the door started to swing toward him, he stepped forward and braced it with his foot.

A moment later, he said, "So, what's the big deal? It's a kitchen. A really ugly kitchen. See?" He swept the room with the light. "No critters, either."

Amy didn't get it.

She pulled him back by his shoulder, allowing the door to begin swinging again.

Then, keeping her own light in the narrowing gap, she exclaimed, "There! See?"

No one spoke.

Like fleeting images caught in the glare of a flashbulb, they saw the room in fragments of frozen white.

And what she saw wasn't the room she had just left.

It wasn't the kitchen.

It was someplace else.

9

Spike slapped a palm against the door and held it open. His light darted around the cupboards and the floor, over the counters and ceiling, but nothing had changed.

"I saw it," Amy insisted shakily. "I don't know. It kind of looked like . . . I don't know." She pushed a shaking hand back through her hair. "It . . . it wasn't the kitchen. I don't know what it was, but it wasn't the kitchen."

"It was an illusion," Becky explained more calmly than she sounded. She flicked her own light on and off rapidly. "See? It happens so fast, you're not sure what you're looking at. Kind of like lightning, you know?"

Maybe, Amy thought reluctantly, but that didn't explain the odd feeling she had also had, that when the door had closed the house had somehow . . . *shifted*.

It was almost like being in a slow-moving car that brakes abruptly—there was the slightest sensation of forward momentum and rocking back, even though she had scarcely moved.

"Enough of this," Spike said. "Upstairs, remember? We've got a timetable to keep."

She shook the feeling off and agreed. It was obvious this place was getting to her. She was spooking herself, and making her friends more unsettled than they already were. She had to get ahold of herself, or the next sound she heard would send her shrieking into the night.

The ludicrous image that thought conjured made her duck her head and smile.

Amy Lowell, woman explorer, racing headlong through Taggard Point, afraid of her own shadow.

Spike released the door to close again on its own, and they hurried back to the staircase. None of them really expected to find anything up there, but they couldn't leave until they knew for sure.

Yet, if Jon wasn't here, then what about the dreams?

No, Amy corrected, the nightmares.

She gripped the newel post and swung herself up. The stairs were bare, and worn in the center, each one creaking ominously when she placed her full weight on it. They turned to the left a dozen steps up; there was nothing on the landing or its facing walls.

"Jon? Hey, Dev?"

Her voice sounded flat, as though the house were absorbing it, refusing to permit it to travel.

"I don't get it. Why don't they answer?" Becky wanted to know.

Spike only grunted, taking the rear and pushing her gently forward.

Amy moved upward slowly, left hand sliding up the dusty banister.

"You know," Spike said, "this would make a great place to come on Halloween."

"Oh, get a life," Becky muttered.

"No, really. Fix it up a little, not too much, put in some colored lights and stuff, get some guys in costumes . . . man, you could scare the—"

Becky . . .

They froze.

Slowly Amy turned back to the foyer.

Becky . . .

"That isn't funny, Spike," Becky snapped.

He shook his head. "I didn't . . . it wasn't me."

Though distant and weak, the voice was clearly Jon's.

Amy leaned over the railing and stared toward the kitchen. Her heart raced for a second when she thought she saw a thin band of light under the first door. She closed her eyes, opened them again, and the glow was still there.

"Guys?"

Becky looked. "But that's . . ." Her hand fluttered. "It was empty."

"Well, it isn't now," Spike said, and dashed down the steps two at a time.

The girls followed, and the three of them slammed

into the room, calling Jon's and Dev's names, and skidding to a halt as the door swung shut behind them.

They couldn't speak.

They couldn't find the words.

The room they had searched earlier had somehow turned to stone. It was so much larger than it had been that they couldn't see the far side. The walls were fashioned of irregular blocks of discolored fieldstone, here and there smeared with what looked like patches of black moss. Clots of dirt and rotting straw were scattered across a rugged stone floor that slanted gently downward toward a small grate set in its center. The soft light came from a large lantern hanging from a rusty chain attached to a hook driven into a dark-wood ceiling beam. There were no windows that any of them could see.

"Man, it's like a dungeon," Spike exclaimed, too amazed to be frightened.

"It's like impossible," Amy answered sharply. "This can't be here."

Then Becky whimpered, grabbed her arm, and turned her around.

The door they had just used had vanished. In its place were two blocks of wood attached to the stone by rusted bolts. And from them hung two thick chains at the end of which were iron bracelets.

Spike, his lips working soundlessly, threw himself against the wall, pushing, prodding, searching for a way out. Then he grabbed the wrench and swung it against the spot where the door had been again and again. There were sparks, but nothing more than the hollow clang of metal against stone. He didn't stop until Amy grabbed his arm and pulled him away, telling him it was no use, they weren't getting out that way.

"Don't be stupid," he snapped. "That's how we got in, isn't it? Doors don't just disappear."

"This one did," Becky said, swallowing hard.

"So what are you saying—we're trapped or something?" He waved her over. "Help me. There's got to be a lever or button or something that triggers it. It's a trick, that's all."

Amy watched their frantic search, but when she tried to use her light to help them, she realized it didn't work. Swearing under her breath, she tapped it several times hard against her leg; nothing happened.

"Don't just stand there, Net," Spike snarled in frustration. "Look around, for God's sake."

She nodded dumbly, and followed the wall to the near corner, grimacing at a slick, sickly sheen on the stone. She touched it with the tip of a finger; it was cool and wet and had no smell. She pushed then, but the stone didn't yield. Then she moved toward the center, leaning slightly forward as she tried to make out what lay on the other side. The lantern was little help; it only turned the distant dark into a shimmering fog.

Then she saw the outline of an exit, caused by flickering light on the other side.

"Hey, guys!"

Water slipped along worn ruts in the stone and trickled through the grate.

"Guys!"

They came running, Becky slipping once and yelping until Spike grabbed her hand. Then they hurried across the room toward a large cell-like door made from bars of iron. She grabbed a rusty metal ring attached to one of the outer bars and pulled. The door was heavy, but it opened smoothly.

"Oh, man," Spike moaned.

A corridor lay on the other side.

A corridor of stone.

Amy checked in both directions, but she couldn't see either end. Torches blazed in brackets every thirty feet along the walls.

"What *is* this place?"

The initial panic subsided into numbness.

By tacit agreement they walked to the right, not finding any other doors or any sign that anyone had been here in years. Ten minutes later, still unable to see the corridor's end, they reversed direction and returned to the cell door.

The air had taken on a faint chill.

The torches writhed, as if touched by a breeze they couldn't feel at all.

"The other way," Amy said, more confidently than she felt.

Becky strode ahead without having to be prodded, her pace swift as she muttered to herself and examined the walls, here smooth and gleaming and flecked with gold mica. Amy stayed close behind, Spike behind her tapping the wrench against his palm, over and over.

They reached a door twenty yards down, solid oak and banded in dark iron, with a wrought-iron latch.

It was locked or jammed; either way, Spike couldn't get it to budge.

Twenty yards farther was a second one. It, too, was locked although there was a judas window at the top through which they could see nothing. It was as dark in there, wherever that was, as midnight without a moon.

Becky had slowed down, and they walked three abreast toward the last door set at corridor's end.

It was wood, like the others, but this one had an ordinary doorknob.

"If it's locked," Becky said angrily, "I'm going to kick the damn thing in."

Amy whirled then, taking a step back the way they had come.

"What?"

She shook her head.

It was a feeling, nothing more, that suddenly they weren't alone.

Someone was back there, hidden in the shifting gloom beyond the reach of the torches.

She almost called out, but something stopped her. Whoever it was, it wasn't Dev or Jon.

"Hey, Net," Spike whispered.

The feeling passed.

The corridor was deserted.

She smiled wanly at him. "It's okay. Nerves, that's all."

"No kidding." He took hold of the knob, closed his eyes briefly, and turned it. "Hey!"

The door opened inward, onto another cell.

Becky shook her head emphatically. "I am not going in there. No way."

"Where else is there?" Amy asked, and stepped boldly over the threshold. This time there was no lantern, but a soft glow without visible source showed her the stone, the wrist and ankle chains, and the splintered beams that ran the length of the ceiling. "Come on, it's empty."

Becky followed so closely, she stepped on Amy's heel, apologized meekly, but didn't move away.

"So where's that light coming from?" Spike asked. "It looks like sun."

Amy agreed. It did indeed look like sunlight, but once again there were no windows.

The room simply glowed.

She heard him move in behind her, and frowned. She checked the floor and the frown deepened.

"Spike?"

"Right here."

"Stamp your foot."

Becky uttered a short, hysterical laugh.

"I mean it. Stamp your foot."

He did, and she spun around just as he released the doorknob. "No!"

He jumped, instinct making him grab the knob before the door completely closed. "What? What?"

This is crazy, she thought; we're all nuts.

"Close the door," she said, "but *don't* let go, okay?"

He didn't ask why. Slowly, so slowly she wanted to scream, he pushed the door shut, keeping the knob turned so the latch wouldn't catch.

And Becky said, "Oh my God."

The moment the door closed, the room changed.

Stone walls became ordinary walls painted white with soft blue trim; the stone floor became Persian carpeting that nearly reached to the baseboards; the beams disappeared, replaced by an ornate tin ceiling etched with grape leaves and flowers. On the opposite wall was a bay window through which sunlight poured through the leaves of a thick-crowned elm just outside.

"Open the door," Amy whispered, not sure whether to laugh or cry or simply give way to the scream that tightened her chest.

Spike did.

The cell returned.

And something large and black lurched toward them from the corner.

10

Amy didn't know which of them screamed, but the noise galvanized Spike into slamming the door and throwing his back against it.

The room changed back.

The creature was gone.

Becky instantly sagged to the carpet and covered her face with her hands. When she looked up, her eyes sparkled with unshed tears. "It's drugs, isn't it?" she asked plaintively.

Amy crouched beside her. "What are you talking about?"

"Yeah, yeah," Spike said, slipping to the floor as well, his hand, however, still firmly gripping the doorknob. "Like, it's in the air, you know? Somebody's pumped some kind of drug inside the house. LSD, something like that." His eyes widened. "Or maybe it *is* the house. All that dust and mold and mildew—maybe just breathing the air is making us see things."

It almost made sense.

Until Becky said, "Then how do we get back?" She stared at Spike. "How do we get home?"

Amy patted her shoulder, then gave it a quick squeeze before moving over to the window. The trunk of the elm was fat and gnarled, and shrubs grew high and closely around it. Through the gaps she was able to see what looked like a meadow, with misted hills in the distance. Tentatively, she poked at one of the small panes. It felt like glass, but when she took out her flashlight and rapped it, it sounded like metal. She rapped it harder. Again. Then slammed the butt into the pane as hard as she could.

The flashlight's plastic casing splintered.

The window remained untouched.

She perched on the edge of the broad sill and tossed the flashlight disgustedly to the floor. If this was really the result of some kind of hallucinogenic drugs, it was the most real illusion she had ever heard of.

Illusions, on the other hand, don't shatter plastic to little pieces; nor, she added as she looked at her hand, do they stab you. A small piece of the casing had scratched the heel of her thumb. She sucked at it absently, ignoring the faint sting as she glanced to her right and saw, barely outlined in the white wall, another door.

She felt the others watching her as she walked over,

leaned close, and saw that the knob was the same color and design.

She took hold.

"Don't," Becky pleaded.

"Amy," Spike said, "No kidding, I wouldn't if I were you."

She opened it.

He closed his eyes.

On the other side was an immense ballroom.

White again, with silver and gold trim, and four teardrop chandeliers hanging evenly spaced along a high-domed ceiling. The hardwood floor shone, and against the walls were dozens of velvet-cushioned chairs.

She opened it wider so they could see, then beckoned. "Come here, Beck."

Becky shook her head. "I'm not moving until this stuff wears off."

"I mean it," she insisted. "Come here. I want to try something."

An idea had begun to scratch at the back of her mind, demanding her attention. It may not be an explanation of what was happening, but it might give them a clue as to how this madness worked.

She pointed at Spike. "Do not, for anything, let go of that door."

He nodded a *don't worry about me, I'm here for life,* then nudged Becky with his foot until she rocked unsteadily to her feet.

"I'm going in there," Amy told her. "All you have to do is close the door behind me—"

"Amy, no, please!"

"—and count to ten. Then open it again, okay?"

She didn't give the girl a chance to protest. She stepped into the ballroom and closed the door quickly, and released the knob.

Before she had a chance to blink, the ballroom became an ordinary room, without furniture or decoration, with an ordinary single window on her right that overlooked a glacier-capped mountain.

It was snowing outside.

When she turned around, the door was gone. The wall was solid.

"Nine, ten . . . please, Becky," she pleaded, feeling her own tears begin to well.

The wall opened, and she charged back into what she knew now was some kind of antechamber for the ballroom. Or would have been in the world she lived in. She dropped heavily to her knees and hung her head, gulping for air, shaking her head as Spike fired one question after another at her until Becky snapped, "Knock it off. It changed, get it? It changed into something else."

Spike shut up, his face pale and drawn.

Amy rubbed at the tension gathering at the back of her neck and stared at the pastoral scene outside the bay window. There was no sign of a mountain, and it was, quite clearly, spring out there.

Wherever *there* was.

She settled back on her heels and blew out a breath, pushed her hair out of her eyes and swiveled around so she could see both of them.

"I think I know," she said.

"Know what?" Spike asked.

"Why it's called the Forever House."

Whatever this thing is, she explained, staring blindly at the ceiling so she could concentrate, the doors are the key. And leaving the kitchen must be the trigger that sets them off. She reminded them of the curious feeling of shifting they had had when the swinging door closed. That was when the Forever House set in motion the maze—for want of a better description—that had snared them.

And that's why it was called the Forever House—because if you didn't find the key, there was no getting out unless you were extremely lucky.

So, there are connected areas, some of them only one room large, some of them . . . who knows, maybe dozens of rooms big. What you have to do is figure out which doors to leave open, and which ones you can safely close, without fear of not getting back to where you began.

They had already closed the door in the dungeon, so they had to find another way out.

But if they tested each room before they entered, they would know which ones to leave open, at least for the time being.

It was confusing.

Leaving a door open might deny them the right path.

But if that thing in the cell was any indication, closing a door might mean . . .

•   •   •

She lay on her back and closed her eyes.

"Panic," Becky said, dropping down beside her.

Amy lifted an eyebrow.

"Whoever built this thing wants you to panic. Like when you're scared out of your skull and you just keep running. You don't think. And even if you do figure it out sooner or later, it's too late."

Amy didn't have to think about it.

It's probably what happened to Jon.

It's probably what happened to who knew how many others who stumbled into this nightmare.

Even a nightmare trimmed in silver and gold.

She looked over at Spike. "You can let go now."

He stared at his hand. "What if it goes away?"

"The only thing back there is the cell. We already know that's a dead end."

He maneuvered around until he was kneeling, and she could tell by the way his shoulders moved that he was taking deep breaths to gather his courage.

Then, slowly, he released the knob.

Nothing happened.

"Yes!" he said, pumping a fist in the air, spun around and said, "But what was that thing we saw?"

"I don't know. But I'll bet it isn't going to be the only thing that lives in here."

He glared at her. "You didn't have to tell me that, you know. Really."

She grinned, and it felt good.

"So now what?" Becky asked.

Amy sat up. "So we prop that other door open and

see what's next." The look on her friend's face made her add, "We really don't have a choice. It's either that, or go back to the dungeon."

"Thank you, no," Spike said quickly. "I'll take my chances out there." He gestured toward the ballroom. "Besides, it seems like it's safe here. If we get into trouble, we can always come back and start again."

They moved to the ballroom entrance, opened the door, and looked in.

"Boy, it's beautiful," Becky said. "Like something you see in the movies."

Amy looked around, thinking she could grab one of those chairs and put it against the door. Then Spike reached into one of his pockets.

"Ta-da!"

She gaped. It was a rubber doorstop.

He shrugged as he placed it, then jammed it under the door with his heel. "I grabbed some from that box. You never know, you know?"

She wanted to kiss him.

She did; and so did Becky, and they laughed when a furious blush spread over his cheeks as he sputtered a protest they both knew was false.

Then they crossed the room to the left-hand wall and without hesitation opened the right side of a pair of high double doors. Another antechamber lay beyond, similar to the first. After testing to be sure the door wouldn't close, they went in, immediately moving to the far wall and the exit they saw there.

Spike reached for the knob.

Amy grabbed his wrist. "It'll change if we close this one."

"How do you know that?"

She pointed at the doorknob. The other was white, like the room, but this was porcelain and painted over with small flowers.

"I get it!" Becky said. "If we look in, it'll be the same, maybe another ballroom or something. But if we close it, it'll change."

"I think so."

Spike shook his head doubtfully. "All right, I guess so. But I'll tell you guys something—this is too easy."

"You worry too much," Amy said, and opened the door.

Another white-and-blue room, the view from its ceiling-high, arched windows the same as before.

"See?"

He wasn't convinced, but he followed them through, refusing to release the knob until he was sure. Then he leaned down to jam another doorstop in, and glanced through to the ballroom.

"Oh my God," he said.

A man stood in the center of the bare floor. He was tall, lean, and wore a tuxedo.

They couldn't tell what he looked like.

They could only see the gun he aimed directly at them.

11

Amy threw herself to one side as Spike slammed the door. Becky shrieked and covered her ears when a muffled explosion resulted in a hole splintering through the door. Spike rolled away and scrambled on his hands and knees to the opposite wall. Another shot punctured the door, and Amy, searching the walls in panic, found this area's exit over on the right. It was only as she dove for it that she realized they were in a plain room, unpainted and paneled in pine.

A third shot, and she yanked the door open, and was nearly knocked off her feet when Becky shoved past her, Spike right on her heels.

"Run!" he cried.

They did.

Down a long, dim corridor whose walls and floor seemed made of polished copper. Their reflections twisted grotesquely, their footsteps hammered sharply, and it was too late to return when Amy understood that the man in evening dress hadn't been aiming to hit them.

He only wanted them to panic.

They ran on.

No breaks in the walls interrupted the smooth surface.

They ran on.

The floor grew uneven, ripples making the way increasingly slippery until they had to slow down before one of them slipped and got hurt.

Amy glanced over her shoulder.

Something moved back there.

It wasn't the man.

"Look," she said, panting.

A dark form swirled at the far end, billowing upward like a thundercloud, filling the hall from ceiling to floor, wall to wall. A strong wind began to blow from its center, keening as it whipped around them, shoving them onward. Spike fell, and the girls hauled him to his feet. Becky's feet slipped from under her, and she slid for several feet before she rolled over and regained her feet.

The cloud began to move.

The wind howled.

The walls vibrated, bulging outward and subsiding as though something was behind it, trying to push through.

The wind knocked Amy to her knees. As much as she wanted to take a second—just a second—to rest and catch her breath, she started to scrabble forward on her hands and knees. Spike yanked her up and supported her with an arm around her waist until she was able to run on her own.

Thunder exploded through the hall, adding to the wind, which had risen from a howl to a shriek.

Splits began to appear in the walls, smoke seeping through to be instantly shredded; the ceiling bulged downward, creaking as if it were made of old wood.

Spike shouted something, but Amy couldn't hear a word, and she couldn't catch up as he and Becky pulled slowly away. A panicked glance over her shoulder showed her the cloud moving closer, flaring now and then with electrical charges that sizzled and cracked against the walls and split them further.

Before she had taken another step, they began to reach out, and one of the charges struck near her heel.

She jumped and ran on, near the limit of her endurance, and sobbed when she was able to see past Becky to the end of the hall.

There was a door.

It was open.

Another charge crackled into spiraling blue sparks overhead, making her duck.

Becky leapt through the doorway, turned, and reached out to her.

A long strip of wall curled down and out just ahead, thick smoke pouring through and blinding her. It was too high to jump over and no room to go around; so, at the last second, she dove and slid under it on her stomach, the acrid smoke making her gag as she hustled to her feet and tried to run on.

But she couldn't see.

Not even the powerful windstorm could dispel the heavy smoke, and she hadn't taken three steps before she slammed into a wall and was knocked, breathless, onto her back.

A glaring red charge exploded in sparks beside her ear; she could smell singed hair.

She rolled over and waved her arms frantically, searching for the wall, hoping to use it to guide her to the exit before the electricity got her, or she was smothered by all the smoke.

Just as she managed to stagger to her feet, someone grabbed her wrist and yanked.

With her eyes filled with burning tears, she screamed and fought to free herself, but the grip wouldn't relent until she was yanked forward again. She spun to her knees, one hand furiously trying to clear her eyes as she realized Spike and Becky were trying to close yet another door.

But the wind wouldn't let them.

The charges turned to lightning.

The smoke turned black.

Although she didn't think she had the strength, she lurched to the door and added her weight to theirs. The floor was slippery, purchase almost nonexistent, but a few seconds' work finally did the trick, and when they were sure it was secure, they slumped to the floor and pressed their backs against the door.

Thunder raged on the other side.

The wind still howled and the door trembled at its power; but it held.

Becky drew her legs up and rested her head on her knees. "I can't," she sobbed. "I can't. I can't."

Spike said nothing; his eyes were wide, but it was clear he saw nothing.

Amy coughed violently, emptying her lungs of the smoke.

We can't win, she thought in an abrupt rush of despair; there's no way, we can't win.

She dried her eyes with the backs of her hands, ran a sleeve under her nose, and let her head fall back against the door. The muted voice of the storm made her think of an animal trapped in a zoo's cage, prowling, always prowling, its growl constantly rumbling in the cavern of its throat.

Curious, though, she thought further. It feels like it's still trying to get in.

As if given a signal, the wind slammed the door sharply, and Becky yelped and wrapped her arms over her head.

Amy reached over her head and pressed her palm to the wood.

It was cold, but not uncomfortable.

Raising herself up slightly, she looked over Becky at Spike, who, in the few short minutes since their escape, had developed smudges under his eyes, appearing much darker because his skin was so bloodless.

"Spike? You okay?"

His head turned slowly toward her. "You got any other stupid questions?"

The door shuddered again.

Becky cried out and scrambled across the floor to the other side, where she huddled beneath an oil painting of a three-masted ship riding a high wave.

Amy blinked.

Suddenly the room snapped into focus—a bedroom, and it was furnished. A twin bed to her left with two stacked pillows and a quilt, a nightstand beside it; a long, low dresser on her right with an oval mirror above it; several oils on the walls papered in green and white vertical stripes. A white globe in the ceiling provided the light. Beside the bed was a window, its drapes pulled.

The wind tried again.

She felt an icy draft slip under the door.

"If that damn wind doesn't get us, that guy'll probably try to shoot us again," Spike muttered bitterly.

Amy looked at him. "Why didn't he?"

"Why didn't he what?"

"Try to kill us."

His smile was humorless. "In case you've forgotten, Net, he did. A couple of times."

"No." She jerked a thumb over her shoulder. "Why didn't he come after us? He had a gun; we don't have anything." Something expanded in her chest, an inexplicable feeling of excitement. "And that . . . that *thing*. It was part of the dungeon place, right? So why didn't it come after us either?"

"Because when we went through the door, it wasn't the dungeon anymore." He didn't say it, but his tone added *stupid*.

She pushed forward onto her hands and knees, staring at the pair of doors that flanked the dresser. Then she pivoted to stare at the door that held the storm in the copper hallway. Without realizing it, she had rocked back onto her heels and was tapping her fingers against her thighs.

"We had to force that door closed."

"So?"

"So . . ."

She stared at him intently, forcing him to think.

When he had it, he jumped to his feet and backed away. "It would have followed us."

She nodded eagerly.

"If . . . if we open it now, that lightning will try to fry us."

"So what?" Becky yelled behind them. "Who cares?"

He turned on her, grinning like a madman. "*It* cares, Beck. *It* cares."

"You're crazy," she said, holding up her palms to keep him away. "You're both nuts."

"Becky, listen," Amy said, dropping in front of her and grabbing her wrists. "Listen to me."

She tried to get away, but Amy wouldn't let her, forcing her arms down until she could barely move.

"Beck, listen, okay? If I'm right, if we're right, whatever it is out there is trying to get in because *we don't belong here*."

Becky refused to meet her gaze, her lips moving

soundlessly, tears still running down her reddened cheeks. Her breath came in painful hitches, but she didn't say anything.

"Try to think, Beck," Amy went on. "When we were in the hall, running, did you see another door? Or anything that might have been a door?"

"No," was the instant answer.

"Maybe," said Spike carefully. "You know . . . maybe."

The door shuddered again, the thunder much louder, more insistent.

"Spike, we have to get out of here," Amy said. "Check those doors, okay?" As he hurried over, she added, "And listen to the wind. It might give us a clue."

Despite her fear, Becky finally raised her head. Amy released one wrist and gently pushed the hair away from her eyes. "You see?" she said. "Do you see?"

Meanwhile, Spike braced a hand against the wall and opened the right-hand door just wide enough to allow him to peek inside. "I can't see anything," he said. "It's too dark." He wrinkled his nose. "But God, it smells like a sewer in there."

Amy stared intently at the other wall.

The storm raged on.

"The other one," she said.

"You got it."

He hurried around the dresser, wincing when his leg caught one of the corners. He grabbed the knob and again, braced his other hand.

Nothing happened.

"Stuck," he said angrily.

"Try again."

Another pull, this one hard enough to make him grunt with the effort, popped the door from its frame.

At that instant, thunder exploded and a furious strike of lightning produced a crack in the far door that ran from top to bottom.

"That's it!" Amy yelled triumphantly.

She yanked Becky to her feet and practically dragged her across the room. Spike had already gone through, and as the storm burst the far door off its hinges, Amy and Becky lunged over the threshold and slammed the door behind them.

They listened then, as the wind tossed the furniture around as if it weighed no more than a feather. Glass shattered. Tendrils of smoke slipped around the door's edges.

Then Amy's heart nearly stopped when a voice behind her said, "Man, what kept you so long?"

12

It was an old room that, given its damp, musty smell, had gone long unused. Illumination was provided by three burning logs set on lion-headed andirons in a small brick fireplace, just enough to see dust in thick layers on a rough-hewn round table and the three chairs placed around it. A set of dull brass fireplace tools sat on the raised flagstone hearth; portraits of stern men in Victorian clothes hung on the wall; an oil lamp with a milky glass base sat on a sideboard against a wall whose paper hung in ragged, stained strips.

Near the hearth there was a cracked leather armchair, and in it sat Jon Vernon.

Becky cried his name, and they ran over, ignoring the renewed fury of the windstorm behind them. Jon was still wearing black, but his sweater had been torn open at the shoulder and his jeans were coated with gray dirt, the cloth of the left leg hanging in tatters from the knee. Under his eyes were puffy, dark circles, and his face was taut and pale.

He winced when Becky threw her arms around him, but endured the embrace for a few seconds before gently pushing her away. "Easy. I'm hurting a little." Then he laughed harshly. "A little, hell. I'm hurting a lot."

It took a while for them to calm down. Then, while Spike dragged the other chairs over, Amy explained how they came to be here . . . and how they had pretty much given up any hope of finding him, or Dev Costello.

"You really think he's here?" Jon asked.

"I'd be willing to bet on it."

"Then he's an idiot." He glowered at the fire.

"He was probably trying to help."

"He's still an idiot."

Amy didn't understand the vehemence of his anger. "What does that make us, huh?" she asked heatedly.

He snapped his head around, but before he could answer, a spasm of pain made him groan and fall back into the chair. A droplet of sweat shimmered on his forehead.

"Sorry," he said at last. "I . . . sorry."

"It's okay," she assured him, avoiding a look at the others. "Don't worry about it. We're here, that's all that matters now."

"Right," he agreed, and told them he had learned the secret of the doors as well. But he had had no chance to use it. Something had been chasing him through the maze of rooms almost since his first step into the dungeon. He didn't know what it was, but he did know that whatever chased him hadn't been human.

During one headlong flight down a long, stone staircase that had appeared in what he had thought was a closet, he had tripped and fallen most of the way to the bottom. At first he believed he had been lucky enough to escape with nothing more than a wicked headache and a few scratches and bruises, but before long his knee began to throb and swell, and he had barely been able to make it in here.

"I don't think anything's broken," he finished wearily. Gingerly he pulled the strips of denim apart. "But it's pretty blown up."

Amy saw a horrific bruise stretching from mid-thigh to mid-shin, and she shuddered. It was a miracle he had been able to make it this far. There may be nothing broken, but something definitely wasn't right. Something like that didn't come from just a bad whack on the leg.

"Yeah," he agreed, seeing her expression. His mouth sagged open and he wiped a hand across it. "I don't suppose any of you guys brought anything to eat?"

"Never thought of it," Spike answered.

"Too bad." He winced again. "Because as far as I can tell, there's nothing to eat or drink anyplace here."

One of the burning logs split open, sending a wash of angry sparks into the flue. They jumped at the cannon sound, then settled again as sap bubbled and hissed in the high, twisting flames.

When the silence grew too loud, Spike asked Jon

what else he had seen, as much to fill them in on the house's secrets as to keep his mind off the pain.

"You wouldn't believe it." He laughed weakly and raised his eyebrows. "Never mind. I guess you would."

Most of the time, at the beginning, he hadn't had much chance to do anything but run. After that, he admitted sheepishly, he had been too scared to take close notice of his surroundings. There had been an incredibly long corridor made of polished green marble, several rooms dripping black water from the ceiling, a place that had a huge pool of thick, red liquid in the center, another place that was hotter than the beach in the middle of July, and one so cold there were icicles and frost on everything in it.

Even the most innocent-looking places weren't so innocent once he had been there a while—one soon swarmed with tiny, brown spiders; another drove him out with smoke seeping through the floorboards.

He had no idea how long he had been in this particular area. He had dragged himself in not long after the fall. The room adjacent was just as filthy and old, and the connecting door had already been ajar. It was the fire that had attracted him, and a chance to sit down. For a long time he'd been feeling alternately hot and cold, parchment dry one minute and covered with cold sweat the next.

"Fever," he added unnecessarily. "This damn knee, I guess."

He slumped back in his chair, his eyes closed, breathing lightly through his mouth.

"The question is, what do we do next?" Becky

wanted to know. She perched on the armrest, one hand shifting to settle on Jon's shoulder.

Spike and Amy exchanged knowing glances at the gesture but said nothing about it. Instead, Spike insisted they had to keep moving. There was little chance now they would be able to find their way out of here except through blind luck or a convenient miracle. However, moving would keep them ahead of that . . . *thing*.

"Unless we run into something else," Jon said without opening his eyes. "Besides," and he gestured helplessly at his injured leg.

"Okay." Amy looked around the room. "We need a crutch or something."

Becky snapped her fingers and hurried over to the hearth. "How about a cane?" She grabbed a flat-headed poker from its stand and brandished it like a dueling sword before stabbing it at the floor and leaning on the grip. "It's not perfect, but it's strong. And we can use it for a weapon." She pulled her flashlight from her pocket. "This sure isn't going to do us much good."

"Genius," Jon said admiringly. Then his face clouded over. "But I don't know if I can."

"What choice do we have?" she answered matter-of-factly, bringing the poker over. "If we stay here . . ." She used it to point toward the copper hall.

As if it had heard her, the wind assaulted the door again, sounding like a giant's angry fist.

But only once.

Then it was quiet again, except for the low crackling of the fire.

With a gesture to keep everybody where they were, Amy stood and began to wander around the room. She couldn't sit any longer. Running blindly through the house as all of them had done, as they had been meant to do, certainly wasn't going to do them any good; in a way, Jon's battered knee was a blessing—it would force them to move slowly, which would, in turn, give them a chance to think ahead if they could.

Unfortunately, she also thought Spike was right— the way things looked so far, a miracle would be the only way they would find their way out.

A lopsided smile briefly touched her mouth—what she needed was a plan.

Without considering what she was doing, she walked into the other room—as Jon had said, a duplicate of the first, but without the fireplace. Its single exit was closed, and pressing an ear against the wood told her nothing.

Only silence waited on the other side.

She wondered then if perhaps the doors they had spotted were, in fact, the only exits to each area. In an old house like this, hidden passages couldn't be ruled out. But except for what she had seen in the movies, she hadn't the vaguest idea how to go about locating one. *If* they existed. *If* she wasn't just grasping at straws.

Enough of that, she told herself; things are confusing enough, don't you think?

Still wandering, she discovered a thick pair of

once-green draperies hidden in the gloom. She grabbed one and pulled it aside, coughing at the cloud of dust that puffed into her face. A casement window lay behind the moldy cloth, and beyond the several small panes she saw a desert. Not the gritty, cactus-pocked high desert of the American West, but the sandy dunes of North Africa. Above, the sky was too bright to look at. There was, as always, no sign of life.

Not only did the house alter its inside, it could alter the outside world as well.

Even if they could get out, they wouldn't know where they were or how to get back to Taggard Point.

Suddenly it all overwhelmed her.

Wherever this house existed—between dimensions or between worlds, in her mind or someone else's—it wasn't home.

Wherever her parents were—to tease her, scold her, encourage her—they weren't here.

It wasn't a game.

Despite her determination, there was a very good chance she was going to die.

13

Amy gripped the narrow sill until her knuckles turned white, and slowly pressed her forehead against the warm glass. Before the first tear fell, a gentle hand gripped and released her shoulder.

"Scary, ain't it," Spike said softly.

She nodded.

"Stupid question I think I heard somewhere before, but—you okay?"

She didn't respond.

He sniffed and leaned back against the sill, hands deep in his pockets. He jingled his change once before he scowled at himself and stopped. "We'll have to do something about Jon soon. He hasn't said anything, but that knee's getting pretty bad, and I don't know any first aid."

She didn't respond.

"Becky found a cradle of kindling. She made like a brace and tied it around his leg. It hurts, but he should be able to walk a little now."

What does it matter, she asked the sand and sky bleached white by the sun; why don't we just clean this place up and stay here until it's over? As long as we don't open the door or do something stupid, we'll probably be safe.

Or as safe as we'll ever be . . . here.

"So what's the plan?"

She had a sudden urge to scream at him, to make him see that there was nothing they could do. Nothing.

It came out as an angry "Huh."

He took her shoulders then and turned her away from the desert view. When she stared stubbornly at the floor, he made a fist around her chin and lifted until she was forced to meet his gaze. "No plan?"

Her expression was her answer.

His hand fell away, his jaw dropped in shock. "But you've got to have a plan, Net."

"Why?" she asked.

He blinked at what, to him, was an incredibly stupid question.

"Why?" she repeated.

"Well . . . well, because you're Amy Lowell, that's why. And Amy Lowell always has a plan. It's like . . ." He looked to the ceiling for inspiration. "It's like one of those forces of nature, you know? Winter storms, hurricanes, high tides, Amy Lowell's plans."

She felt an unwanted giggle bubbling in her chest.

"I mean," he went on, waving one hand grandly,

"what would happen to the world as we know it if Amy Lowell didn't have some kind of stupid plan? God, just thinking about it is scarier than this place. Think of it—governments will fall, Alaska will melt, and—" He deepened his voice and dipped his head so they were almost nose to nose. "—Mrs. Samson will leave the classroom and take over the world." He frowned. "Do you really want that responsibility on your shoulders? Children will hate you, you know. Mothers will tell stories about you at night, and they'll make masks of you for Halloween."

She raised her head until their noses did touch. It was a long time before she could speak without her voice cracking. "You're awful, you know."

"Yeah. That's what my mom tells me." He blinked slowly. "My eyes are going to cross."

Reluctantly she leaned back, wondering for a moment just who this guy was. Until tonight—if it was still tonight on the outside—he had been her buddy, hanging around so much there had been times she'd wanted to scream at him to get lost.

And a buddy shouldn't make her feel as awkward as she suddenly did.

A quick check to be sure the desert was still out there, and she said, very quietly, "Thanks, Spike."

He shrugged. No problem.

Then she moved to the room's other exit and, gesturing him to stand behind her, she opened the door a crack—a third room in the same style and the same state of disrepair, except this one was narrow and much longer, and had a refectory table in the middle of the floor.

"Man, you could feed an army at that thing," Spike said.

She opened the door all the way, and looked back toward the fireplace. Becky stood beside Jon's chair, helpless to ease the pain so clear even from here.

"He could lie on the table," she told Spike. "Until we figure out what to do next."

Spike agreed, and together they helped Jon into what she called the dining hall. Once on his back, Jon sighed in great relief, while Spike yanked rotted draperies off high, arched windows. With the best pieces he could find, he fashioned a thick pillow to place under Jon's head.

The desert was still out there, but the explosion of fresh light made the room much less depressing.

Until she saw a glimmer of white in the far corner, untouched by the desert's glare. The distance was too great for her to see exactly what it was, but she had a sinking feeling it wasn't going to be pleasant.

Glancing over her shoulder, she made sure the others were still occupied at the table, talking to Jon and fussing with the makeshift pillow. Then she ambled as casually as she could around the floor, narrowing the gap between her and the corner until she was able to see it more clearly.

A surge of bile rose in her throat.

They were bones.

Human bones.

Before she could stop herself, she dropped to her

knees and stared. Strips of colorless cloth covered most of them, but she recognized part of a shirt and what was left of a pair of trousers or jeans. The way the bones were arranged, it seemed as if the person had fallen here and maybe had curled up, probably to sleep. The skull was turned to the wall.

At first she concluded whoever it was had died of thirst or starvation, and Jon's comment about the lack of food and water suddenly became all too ominous, all too prophetic, and she shook it away.

That's when she realized the skull wasn't attached to the neck vertebrae. That was when she saw the deep gouge in the floorboard.

Oh, God, she thought. He must have been sleeping, and someone cut off his head.

The bile rose and subsided again, leaving a sour taste behind that repeated swallowing couldn't banish. But it was evident this had happened a long time ago, and she reminded herself that this body was the first sign anyone else but them had ever been here.

It wasn't much of a comfort.

In fact, she thought wryly, it isn't any comfort at all.

Nevertheless, curiosity swiftly overcame her initial revulsion, and she leaned closer, reaching out a finger to poke tentatively at the rib cage. The skeleton shifted. She rubbed her nose, reconsidered, and did it again. This time, one of the hands turned over, and she bit back a startled cry, pressing a palm to her chest to keep her heart in place.

Then she noticed a faint wink of gold, and she peered more closely at the hand.

There was a signet ring on one finger.

She reached for it, hesitated, snatched her hand back and rubbed it hard against her leg.

Come on, she scolded; they're only bones, they're not going to bite.

With her lower lip drawn between her teeth she reached out a second time. Her thumb and forefinger gripped the ring tightly, and after several failures, she used her free hand to steady the wrist and slipped the ring easily away.

She shuddered as she sat back, and swiveled toward the window so she could examine the jewelry better.

A signet ring, as she'd thought, and it looked like—

"Oh, no," she whispered. "Oh, no."

She wanted to stand but her legs wouldn't work; she wanted to call her friends, but she couldn't find her voice; and at last her arms dropped heavily to her sides.

She was too numb to be afraid, and too numb to think.

Hurried footsteps turned her head, and she watched dully as Becky approached, slowed when she saw the white pile, and stopped when she realized what the pile was.

"Oh, gross," was all she said, making a face. She looked down at her friend. "Amy, what's the matter? It's only a—hey, what's that?"

Amy didn't move.

"Come on, what've you got there?"

Wordlessly Amy held up her find.

Frowning puzzlement, Becky took it and held it up, turning it around until she saw the faceted glass ruby on top, and the Beachland High School motto inscribed around the octagonal gold crown. Her lips moved silently as she read it, then she brought it over to the window so she could see the inside of the band more clearly.

"Oh," she said when she deciphered it and turned around. "Oh, Amy, no."

Amy finally managed to get to her feet. She didn't want to know, not really, but she walked over anyway and took the ring. When she saw the personal message that had been inscribed there, she cleared her throat several times before she was able to call Spike over.

"What?" he said when he joined them. "Treasure?"

Becky showed him.

"Aw . . . man," he finally said. "Oh, man, this is the pits."

They had found Dev Costello's brother.

14

The despair Amy had felt earlier slowly gave way to a rage that nearly blinded her. She had not known Dev's brother, but the fact that the Forever House had somehow caused his death made her feel so powerless that the rage increased.

While Spike covered the bones with the rest of the drapery he had pulled down and Becky told Jon about their discovery, Amy prowled the room's perimeter, occasionally punching the wall, kicking it, swearing at it, until she had made four complete circuits. By then, she had calmed down.

But the rage remained.

Before, the notion that she would probably die in here had been an abstraction. A momentary surrender to the fear that clung to her like a cloak, settling and billowing, sometimes holding her back.

Now it was a reality.

Somehow, in a way she didn't really understand, that made dealing with it easier.

That made fighting it vital.

Spike was right: she needed a plan.

It was too late to attempt a map of the house, and the more she thought about it, the more she became convinced it would be useless anyway. The house, or whatever controlled it, didn't seem to have any rhyme or reason. Nor, when she thought about it further, did it seem specifically attuned to them—they, or their minds, weren't able to dictate what each new set of rooms would look like. It was, at the end, all based on whim, as far as she could tell.

Luckily, they had stumbled into Jon, but she couldn't count on luck staying with them all the time.

They still hadn't seen any sign of Dev.

A few minutes later she found herself facing the windstorm door.

It was silent out there as well, and no smoke leaked around the edges.

The thing was gone, just like the man who had shot at them.

She stepped back.

The man.

She had forgotten about him in all the excitement.

A finger drifted to her lips. And what about that creature they had seen in the cell? Huge, dark, and no doubt deadly, it hadn't come after them once they'd left its domain. Nor had the armed man.

But the wind had.

From that, she already guessed she wasn't supposed to be here; the question was, why?

What was so important about this particular area that made the house go after them so desperately?

Of course, this would all be a lot easier if she could find a cryptic message scrawled on the wall from a previous traveler, or on a scrap of paper hidden in some compartment or under a chair or behind a loose brick in the fireplace. As long as you're at it, she told herself as she trailed her fingers along the wall, why don't you just ask for a crystal ball or a lamp with a genie waiting inside to transport you back to the Point?

She passed the fireplace, absently picking up the ash shovel as she went and propping it on her shoulder like a baseball bat. The desert still glared from the window, the drapery was still pale with age and dust, and there in the corner by the door to the dining hall . . .

She gaped.

Quickly she reached for her flashlight and remembered with a groan that she'd smashed it against the window. A call for Spike brought him running.

"Shine your light there," she said, pointing at a section of the wall about two feet from the floor.

He pulled it from his hip pocket. "They don't work, remember?"

She sagged. "I forgot."

"Why? What's up?"

She told him she thought she had seen some scribbling on the wall, but it was too dark to make out. He aimed the flashlight anyway and thumbed the switch up.

The light came on. It was weak, the bulb barely glowing, but it was on.

Excited and speechless, they crouched as close as they could, Spike holding the light almost against the wall while Amy tried to make out the words.

"What does it say?"

With a disappointed sigh she shook her head and straightened. "Nothing. It's just dirt, that's all." She shrugged with one shoulder. "Sorry."

"Hey, that's okay, I—"

He stopped and cocked his head.

"Spike?"

He hushed her and turned slowly, one hand up to keep her silent.

For a long moment she couldn't figure out what he was listening to, and was about to ask, when she heard it—a distant rumbling and, a few seconds later, an equally distant high-pitched keening.

Before she could say anything, the storm crashed into the door so violently that the entire room shook and dust fell in pattering veils and streaks from the walls and ceiling. She grabbed his arm, and they hustled into the other room where Jon had sat up and was holding Becky's hand. Explanations were unnecessary.

Again the wind exploded, and the firelight flickered madly, dancing manic shadows across the floor and walls.

"We've got to get out," Jon said, struggling to get off the table.

Becky made to push him back, but his leg did it for

her, a spasm of pain causing him to stiffen, his neck muscles taut, his left arm gripping his thigh so tightly the blood left his fingers. When it passed, he let her ease him onto his back where he stared at the ceiling, gulping for air.

The episode didn't last more than a minute or two, but it seemed like hours.

And when it was over and an uneasy quiet had returned, Spike went back to the first room and examined the door. Amy saw him shake his head as he pressed against the wood, then ran his hands over the wide hinges. He stepped back, stared, then grabbed one of the chairs and propped it under the doorknob.

"I don't think that'll do much good," he said once he'd returned to the dining hall. "But it's all I can think of. Those hinges have nearly pulled out of the frame."

"And when it gets in?" Becky asked.

"Don't ask," he answered glumly. He leaned over Jon. "How you doing, man?"

"Moved too fast."

"Think you can walk?"

Jon gave him a lopsided grin. "Do I have a choice?"

"Nope. I was just being polite."

Becky brushed some hair away from Jon's brow. "What happened in there?"

"I don't know," Amy said. She told her how she had thought she'd seen some writing on the wall and Spike had used the flashlight to help her see. Not that it worked very well. Just enough to prove Amy had been indulging in wishful thinking. Before they could do anything, the storm had attacked.

Becky glanced fearfully around the room. "Maybe we made it mad."

"How did we do that?" Spike asked. "All we did was look around, for crying out loud."

"No," Amy said. She started pacing again. "No."

"What do you mean, 'No'?"

She slashed the air with her hand to shut him up. She had to think. An idea hovered just out of reach, and she needed time to draw it closer, to have a good look. Suddenly she whirled and slapped the table with a palm. "Got it!"

"Got what?"

"I'm not totally sure, but I think I've got a way we might have a chance of getting out of here."

She boosted herself onto the table and sat cross-legged at Jon's feet. She wished she had more time to think things through, but despite Becky's clever handiwork, Jon needed real medical attention. All she could do was hope she was right, or close enough to it that she wouldn't get them all killed.

"Remember what happened when we ran into that cell?"

"Sure," Spike said. "We ended up in this nightmare."

"I don't mean that."

Becky didn't get it.

"The flashlights went out, remember? There was only that lamp or something hanging from the ceiling."

"Okay. So what?"

"They're working now."

"The batteries are weak, that's all," Jon said.

"No, they're not." Spike took his out and slapped it against his palm. "Dad always keeps fresh batteries in them. For when the electricity goes or something." He grinned. "He has this thing about the dark."

Amy leaned over. "And this house has a thing about them."

Becky rolled her eyes. "You're not making any sense."

"Think about it for a minute, okay? That storm thing, whatever it is, chases us in here, right? We're not supposed to be in here, right? But it leaves us alone until Spike turned on the flashlight again."

"Now wait a minute," Becky protested. "Are you trying to tell me that thing is alive?"

"It knows, right?"

Becky wouldn't concede the possibility. It was too outlandish, even for this place.

But when they heard the thunder rumbling in the hall, prowling, biding its time and perhaps gathering its strength, Amy couldn't help it:

"Yes," she said. "I think it's alive."

15

"Coincidence," Jon scoffed. "It's nothing but coincidence. You better come up with something else, Net. This stuff isn't getting us anywhere."

"Turn it on, Spike," she said.

He stared at the flashlight. "I don't know. If you're right, I'm not sure that door'll hold."

"If nothing happens, I'm wrong, and we don't have anything to worry about."

He shook his head doubtfully.

"Oh, for God's sake," Becky snapped. She hauled out her own flashlight and switched it on. The beam, as before, was virtually nonexistent.

And as before, the storm exploded in the hall.

They stared through the doorway to the first room, holding their breath as the chair shuddered under the assault, as ribbons and showers of dust fell from the walls and ceilings, as the whole floor trembled, moving the table with it.

Immediately, Becky shut it off and dropped it on the table as if it had bitten her.

The storm subsided, though not as quickly as before.

When silence returned, they stared at Amy, amazed.

"I don't know if this place is run by magic or what," she explained, plucking at her jeans. "All I know is, once that kitchen door closes, the inside goes someplace else. A hundred, maybe a thousand different places. Who knows? You look through the windows, and it's always different out there. And out there isn't the Point."

Her left hand massaged the back of her neck.

"Well?" Spike said impatiently. "Go on."

Becky braced her hands on the table. "Wait a minute, give her a chance, huh? I think what she's saying is that there are some . . . rooms, I guess, that are closer to the Point than others?"

"Yes!" Amy said with a sharp nod. "I mean, everything we've seen in here is either really old, or really old-fashioned. So maybe that's why the flashlights don't work all the time. But the closer we get—"

"The brighter they shine!" Spike exclaimed.

Jon propped himself up on his elbows, disgusted. "You guys are nuts."

"So is this place," Spike countered. "You got a better idea?"

Jon glared at him, but said nothing. He lowered

himself back to the drapery pillow and laced his fingers across his stomach.

"So we check out each room," Amy said, unfolding her legs and jumping down to the floor.

"The flashlight doesn't work, we don't go in," Becky added with a smile.

"And if it does, we do," Spike finished.

"Anybody figure out what we do if those flashlights never get any brighter than they are now?" Jon wanted to know.

"Considering the alternative," Spike told him, "who cares? At least we're doing something."

Without further debate, the girls moved quickly to the farthest door, near the corner where Spike had covered Matt's remains. They gave each other a *good luck* look, then Amy opened the door and Becky looked inside.

"Too dark," she said.

"The light, dope." Amy gave her a little push. "You may have to cross over."

"Not in this life," she muttered. Instead, she slapped a hand around the jamb. "There's a wall right here." She tested the other side. "Here, too." She pushed against the door until Amy moved out of the way to let the sunlight in. "Swell. A closet."

"The flashlight," Amy reminded her. "It may not really be a closet, you know. When the door's closed . . ." She shrugged, and eased the door over until there was just enough room for Becky to stick in her arm and head. "Well?"

"Nope. No light."

"Then it's the other one." But she crossed her fingers, just in case.

The bulb glowed faintly.

The room seemed to be an extension of the dining hall, but Amy had a feeling that would change once they were inside. Meanwhile, Spike eased Jon off the table, handed him the poker, and made him put his arm around his waist for support. It was awkward going, but they made it across the floor without too much trouble.

"We'll go as fast as we can," Amy told them. "We'll only stop when Jon really needs it."

"Big of you," he muttered.

"Hey," Spike snapped. "What's your problem?"

"Later," Amy said impatiently. "Let's get it over with."

She stepped in first. Becky followed the boys and, holding her breath, pulled the door shut.

The Forever House *shifted*.

A spartan room with no decoration or furniture at all. It was barely eight feet square. Nothing but wood, worn and pale, and a nearly overpowering stench that made them all gag. It had a single round window from which Amy spotted a lush and steamy forest, all the trees like giant ferns, and the underbrush so thick she couldn't see the ground at all.

The only thing different between this view and the

others was the vague sense that something out there was looking in at her.

Again, there were two doors.

Again, Becky found the one that allowed the light to glow.

The Forever House *shifted*.

A cavern so vast they couldn't see the walls, could not tell how high the roof was.

Deep in the shadows, water dripped monotonously, and green patches of phosphorescence glowed faintly here and there, providing them with enough light to guide them around the perimeter. Pools of stagnant water bubbled and steamed. Their footsteps echoed like gunshots no matter how softly they tried to walk. They searched dozens of alcoves before they found an exit. Then, while Jon sat on a flat-topped low boulder, Spike and Becky continued on, finding two more before they had completed the circuit.

The second one let the light glow.

It didn't seem any brighter.

shifted

A narrow cave of rock ledges, the roof so low they had to make their way through in a crouch. The green glow had changed to yellow. A bloated rat scurried along a chest-high ledge, teeth bared and red eyes glaring. In a shallow depression they found another pile of bones, most turned to dust, and it was clear more than one person had died there. Water dripped. Slime covered the ground, forcing them to move even slower.

Spike banged his skull on a bulge of overhead rock. Slightly stunned, he almost collapsed to his knees, but Jon managed to hold him up until his head and vision cleared.

"We should have stayed in the other place," Jon complained.

"And end up like Matt?" Becky said.

Amy frowned as she picked her way across the slippery ground. She didn't understand what was wrong with Jon. The pain, surely, had something to do with it, but he was acting almost as if he didn't want to leave. Other than the tuxedo man and, possibly, the storm, that rat was the only other living creature they had encountered, and she couldn't see spending the rest of her life in a dusty room. Waiting for the windstorm to kill. Waiting to starve to death.

"Take it easy, man," Spike whispered to him then.

Jon's response was unintelligible, but it sounded like an apology to her.

The pain, that's all; it was the pain.

"This is more like a tunnel," Becky said a few minutes later. She slipped then, and snapped out one hand to keep from falling all the way. "Oh, gross."

Two exits side by side greeted them when they finally reached the far wall.

In one Amy could hear the soft sound of fluttering wings.

Bats, she thought, suppressing a shudder, and prayed the flashlight wouldn't work in there.

It didn't.

shifted

A wrought-iron, spiral staircase wound downward through a cobblestone floor.

Although Jon didn't think he could make it, Spike showed him how to use cane and banister to safely take all the weight off his leg. If that didn't work, he could go down on his rump.

"Great," said Jon.

"You want to rest?" Becky asked.

"No. Let's get going."

It was only wide enough for one at a time. Amy again took the lead, Jon behind her, then Spike and Becky. She couldn't see what lay below the floorline, and it took her a few seconds to take that first step.

She couldn't see a thing.

Now there was no light, no glow, nothing at all.

They'd be descending into total black.

Keeping a firm grip on the twisted banister, she moved on, testing each step, straining to make some sense of the dark that surrounded her. She paused once, and reached out with her free hand to see if she could touch a wall; she touched nothing, and had a sudden, stomach-wrenching feeling that the bottom of the staircase was hundreds of feet away.

If it had a bottom at all.

Now that's dumb, she thought as she took the next

step; it had to have a bottom. How could it stand otherwise?

How else, she wondered, could the Forever House exist?

She tried counting the steps taken, and stopped at fifty.

The only sound, other than their breathing, was the metallic tap of the poker's tip against each step.

Spike took some change out of his pocket and dropped it over the side.

They didn't hear it land.

Jon finally demanded a rest, and Amy, though she bridled at his tone, didn't argue. Her legs were trembling with the effort not to run, and she sagged onto her step gratefully.

"I have to see," Spike said, his voice thin in the dark.

"Not a good idea," Becky warned.

"But I feel like I'm blind."

Amy understood. The total darkness was deceptive— one minute, it gave her an almost comfortable feeling of enclosure, and the next it made her feel as if she no longer had any control over her balance. If she let go of the banister, she just knew she would fall.

The flashlight winked on.

Amy gasped.

It was much brighter.

"Hey," he said admiringly. "Pretty good, Net."

He aimed the beam downward first, but all they saw were more steps spiraling into the black; and while it didn't reach very far when he swung it over the side, Amy thought she saw a suggestion of a wall.

Spike leaned over Jon and tapped her on the shoulder. "Here." He gave her the flashlight. "So you can see when we're at the bottom."

As soon as she took it, Becky said, "Turn it off!"

Amy did without thinking about it.

But it was too late.

The staircase began to vibrate as something, or someone, began climbing down from above.

16

"Move!" Jon whispered harshly. He handed the poker to Spike. "Come on, Amy, move it!"

She hesitated only a second before starting down, her palm burning as it slid along the uneven iron banister, her feet no longer bothering to test for support. When she glanced back, she saw Jon using his hands to brace himself on each step before practically throwing himself down to the next one. His face was red with exertion, his mouth open to breathe, and it didn't take long before she realized she shouldn't be able to see any of that at all.

She frowned, wondering what new thing the house had conjured for them, until she saw a bright light pulsing far below her, casting convoluted shadows of the staircase against the walls.

Unhurried footsteps rang through the stairwell, behind them, in the dark.

A muffled curse came from Becky when her foot slid off a step and she had to grab the banister with both hands to keep from tumbling into Spike. Jon chanted, "Go! Go!" in a dull monotone each time he reached a new level. Spike, face flushed and gleaming with sweat, visibly had to force himself not to vault over his friend.

"You needn't hurry, children," a deep voice called, mockingly sweet.

Amy moved faster.

The glow intensified.

When she stumbled and nearly fell, she realized the staircase had begun to sway, and a tortured creaking terrified her into greater speed as the braces that held the steps to its central pole protested the extra pressure.

An angry cry told her Jon had somehow banged his leg, but she couldn't stop to help; her downward momentum had increased, and it was all she could do now to keep from pitching over the side as the staircase's swaying increased as well.

"You needn't hurry at all."

Only a few steps more, a dozen or so, she told herself as she descended swiftly into a cloud of light so glaringly bright she became nearly as blinded as she had been in the dark. Her free hand shaded her eyes so she wouldn't miss a step. A glance upward showed her Jon still moving as best he could, with Spike and Becky close behind.

"Why don't you rest, children? Why not stop and rest?"

She reached the bottom, and staggered immediately across a hardwood floor toward an open doorway, her only thought to escape that mocking voice.

Harsh laughter filled the stairwell.

Amy caught herself just before panic drove her across the threshold into the untested room, whirling as Jon reached the floor and hauled himself to one foot, blinking sweat from his eyes. Spike came right behind him, grabbed his waist and pulled him close. With the glare in her eyes, they looked like dark ghosts.

"The flashlight!" Spike yelled.

Amy turned it on.

The laughter rolled over them, sounding too much like thunder.

"Hurry!" he urged.

Nothing happened when she stretched her arm through the doorway, and she froze with indecision because she couldn't see any other way out. Then Becky, when she saw her way blocked by the boys, vaulted the banister several steps from the bottom, landed on hands and knees, and yelled triumphantly, "Here! Over here!"

She spotted it herself then, the vague outline of an exit behind the staircase itself. Becky reached it first, her hands running over the surface, searching for a latch, a knob, anything at all. "No!" she cried in frustration, and kicked viciously at the bottom.

The door flew open.

Before she could move, Spike dragged Jon through, she followed close enough to trip over their heels, and Amy was left alone for the moment.

Listening to the footsteps.

Listening to the laughter.

"Who are you?" she couldn't help screaming, trying to see up the staircase.

The voice answered patiently, "You know."

Automatically she raised the flashlight like a club, thinking she might be able to catch the tuxedo man—it could have been no one else—before he saw her, perhaps stun him long enough for her to escape.

But the footsteps were too loud.

The renewed laughter too coated with evil.

She bolted after her friends, waving a desperate hand in front of her as if that might somehow clear a way through the blinding light. And once she was in the other room, featureless and white, she spotted the others slipping through an exit to her left.

"Wait!" she called.

They didn't stop.

She sprinted after them, but before she reached the doorway something stopped her, and she turned.

"Oh my God," she whispered.

It was the white room of her nightmare.

The realization immobilized her, and she could only turn her head slowly when a dark figure stepped calmly out of the cloud of bright light.

He was quite tall, quite good-looking, his evening

wear fitting him as if he were born to it. Thick black
hair was brushed straight back across his scalp from a
sharp widow's peak, and a distinguished dusting of
gray marked him at his temples. When he looked at her
as though from a height much greater than it was, his
thin red lips parted slowly in an infuriating, satisfied
smile. His eyes were deep-set and black, but they
didn't smile at all.

Amy gaped, still unable to run, barely able to
breathe.

"Amy, help me, I'm lost," he said.

With a gasp of recognition, she heard it as if in a
distant dream: *Amy, help me, I'm lost.*

Jon's voice, pleading in her nightmare.

It hadn't been Jon at all.

Without daring to take her gaze from his face, she
backed away, a sudden cold finger scratching at her
heart. "Who *are* you?"

He folded white-gloved hands in front of him and
shook his head in a mild scolding. "I'm ashamed of
you, child. Don't you recognize me?"

His voice, though deep, was as smooth and hypnotic
as flowing black water.

She shook her head in emphatic denial.

He glanced around the white room, shaking his head
sadly. "And you've learned so much." His chest rose
and fell in a sigh. "What a pity you're not as clever as
I'd thought."

She took another careful step back. "Why are you
doing this to us?" Despite her best efforts, her voice
broke. "Why don't you leave us alone?"

"Child, you know I can't do that."

"Stop calling me that!"

He nodded graciously. "Very well." The smile broadened. "Amy."

God, this isn't happening, she thought wildly; this can't be happening. He can't know who I am. He can't. I've never seen him before.

He held out a gloved hand. "Come along, Amy Lowell. Come along with me now, and I promise you, on my honor, you won't feel a thing."

She wavered.

That voice . . . it coiled around her mind, cold and warm at the same time.

"Come, Amy."

She looked down in horror as her left leg moved forward, and her right leg followed. She tried to stop, but she couldn't control her limbs. She tried to scream for help, but her throat wouldn't work.

"Come."

He wasn't so bad actually, when she thought about it. Not really. He was kind of handsome in a regal sort of way. It wouldn't surprise her if he revealed that he was a count or a duke.

"Come."

And if this was the white room in her nightmare, then this scene was obviously just an extension of that dream.

With great effort she looked over her shoulder. "Don't worry. They'll be fine. Come to me, Amy. It's much better this way."

They'll be fine?

Even as she took another involuntary step, she frowned.

They?

Her eyes widened, and the serpentine coil snapped and freed her legs. Her arms stretched outward for desperate balance as she stumbled backward as though struck in the chest, and her shoulder collided with the doorjamb, the quick painful stab clearing her mind.

"Amy." He became stern. "Amy."

"How many?" she asked then.

His head tilted in silent question.

"How many have you killed?"

The smile vanished.

"Not nearly enough," he answered, and started toward her. His hands slipped to his sides, his expression hardened. "Not nearly enough."

17

Before she knew what she was doing, Amy reared back and heaved the flashlight at his head. His hand snapped up to ward off the unexpected attack, and as soon as the flashlight smacked into his palm, he was forced to step back.

The Forever House *shifted*.

Amy felt the familiar nausea rise as her vision slightly blurred. She clamped a hand to her stomach and spun into the next room, ran across the floor and through the open exit on the other side.

She heard nothing behind her.

She saw none of her friends, but she didn't dare stop, and when she called out, there was no answer. All she had were the doors she hoped would lead her to them.

Another door, then, and a stone archway, and a pair of bat-wing doors that swung away when she approached, and swung back when she ran through, into a long, green marble corridor that must have been the one Jon had passed through.

A single door at the far end opened before she reached it, giving her access to a place much like an auditorium without a stage at the back. She wasted precious time searching the rows and aisles for her friends, then chose a glass door on the left that looked as if it led to the outside.

It led to a bedroom decorated all in pink.

Which led to a rotted-wood room that smelled of blood and death.

Another corridor, short and wide, that was cold enough to allow her to see her breath.

"Where are you?" she yelled. "Spike! Becky!"

Four doors covered with frost burned her hands when she tried to open them. For a panicked second she thought she was finally trapped, but chips of ice on the floor by one made her sob with relief; it was a clear indication someone had gone this way.

She used her shoulder to force it open, stumbling into a featureless room whose floor slanted toward the back. She slipped, fell, and slid through the half-size exit feet first, scrambled up, and saw a solitary door half-open on the left.

She had no choice; she ran through it.

Into a room painted completely red.

Amy, help me

The spiderweb was in the corner, just as she had

seen it. And from the size of it, she didn't want to meet the creature that had spun it—it stretched from floor to ceiling, wall to wall, beads of moisture glittering like jewels on all of the strands. At its foot were scattered husks of insects, and larger husks of animals she could almost identify.

I'm lost

She stifled a cry when she recognized one of them was a large dog.

A dry rustling sound made her look up, and she saw a fat shadow slipping across the ceiling overhead, and heard a faint chittering noise.

She ran, nearly weeping as her feet came down on other husks she hadn't noticed, crunching them like dead leaves until she flung herself through a doorway that opened on a polished wood hallway whose floor had a royal blue runner stretched down its center. The walls were lined with glass cases on either side; they were empty, save for piles of rags coated with brown dust lying on the bottom.

Above her, chandeliers bounced softly in an unfelt breeze.

She ran on, having no choice but to follow the hall as it curved to the right and rose in an easy slope toward three doors at the top.

Each door was framed in red velvet tied back with silver cord, each with a large gold disc embossed with stars affixed over the lintel.

And all of them were open.

She slowed as she neared them, frantically trying to determine which one the others had chosen. Quickly she moved from one to the other, peering in, seeing nothing, until a sob escaped her when she realized it was impossible.

She couldn't know.

They were gone.

Her arms flapped helplessly at her sides as she examined each doorway again. There *had* to be a way. After all this time and all she had been through, it couldn't end like this. She wouldn't let it.

"Child."

She whipped around.

He wasn't in sight, but she could hear his footsteps even on the carpeting, taking his time, confident she wouldn't be able to escape him again.

"Child."

"No, please," she whispered.

Okay, she thought; okay, it's the middle one. No. The right one. No.

Yet each time she decided on a direction, something stopped her.

It was him, she realized, trying to snare her again with the web of his voice.

"Child."

The footsteps came closer.

She was about to give up and simply thrust herself through the nearest exit and take her chances on what she found, when something glittered faintly at the corner of her vision. After a moment's indecision, she rushed over to the right-hand doorway, leaned over, and stared.

It was a quarter lying just over the threshold.

"Amy."

Oh, God, thank you, Spike, she mouthed at the ceiling, snatched the coin up, and charged inside.

She hadn't taken more than half a dozen steps when she skidded to a halt.

She was in a place not much larger than her own bedroom. Except for a mirror propped against the opposite wall, it was empty.

It was painted completely black.

There were no exits.

Once again she had been tricked; once again despair flooded over her, and she dropped heavily to her knees in disbelief and anguish.

"No use," she muttered. "No use. It's no use."

She was weary of running and fighting, all her strength gone at last, and the tears she had forced herself not to shed were finally released, cascading down her cheeks as she choked on every sob.

No use, she thought. No use.

Her hands lay limply on her thighs. Her neck no longer had the power to hold her head up. It seemed as if every muscle in her body ached or burned and demanded she rest.

Maybe the man, whoever he was, was right. Maybe it was finally time she surrendered to the inevitable. At least nobody could say she hadn't given it her best shot. The plan had been a good one, but like the water balloon in the park, this one had misfired too.

And if this awful night had taught her anything, she knew it was too late to think of another.

Though her tears had finally stopped, another sob stung her throat, and her right hand folded into a tight, impotent fist, nails digging harshly into the heel of her thumb . . . and something else that sparked a touch of fire at the base of one finger. She opened her eyes, uncurled her fingers, and saw the quarter lying in her palm.

At first she didn't realize what it was and only stared at it dumbly.

Then: "Oh." She sniffed and passed a sleeve across her eyes and under her nose. "Oh!"

Although a cramp threatened one of her calves, she rocked to her feet quickly, swayed for a moment until the near-cramp passed, then retreated to the door and walked slowly around the empty room. She pushed against the walls as high and low as she could reach in case a hidden exit worked on a spring or balance mechanism. When that failed, she trailed her fingers over the cold smooth wood, searching for telltale signs of gaps and edges or recessed latches in the smooth black surface. And when that failed too, she slapped a scolding hand against her forehead and walked over to the mirror.

It was exactly as she had dreamed it—thickly coated with granular dust. The ornate frame was glided wood carved in intricately twisting spirals. She gripped it on either side, and tried to move it aside. When it didn't budge, she dropped to her knees and tried to pull one side far enough away from the wall so she could see behind it. There had to be an exit there, a hole of some kind; it was the only place left, and she should have thought of it right away.

The frame didn't move.

She backed off to the room's center.

There was no place else to search; there was nothing left to try.

As impossible as things had already been, this was . . . impossible. Spike had left the coin for her to find, a signpost pointing straight in here.

So where had they gone?

Then she looked up so quickly, she nearly wrenched her neck. Then she sighed.

Nothing; not a trapdoor, nor a gap . . . nothing.

The floor was the same.

There was only one way in.

There was no way out.

The voice was distant, but clear:
Child, i'm coming

18

She almost lost control.

The voice, like a serpent hissing in a dream, slipped into the room almost as if it were a visible thing.

Swallowing a rush of fear, ordering herself not to panic, she crept to the doorway, took a deep breath, and looked down the length of the corridor to its curve. The chandeliers had stopped their swaying; the glass cases had filled with billowing yellow fog.

She couldn't see him.

But he was on his way.

"All right," she whispered, using her own voice to calm herself down. "Okay. All right."

He had tried to seduce her into giving up, using that voice and those eyes even when he wasn't present. That much she had already figured out.

"Okay."

Oddly enough, however, when she actually heard him, it only made her madder.

"Come on, you dope, think!"

She took hold of the door's edge as if to slam it shut, but caution and experience stopped her, demanding she consider what might happen, and what would certainly happen if she didn't take charge.

If she closed it, the odds were pretty good the room would change, just like the others, and she would find herself somewhere else in this hellish house; and her friends would very likely be lost to her forever.

But if she closed it and the room stayed the same, as happened with the ballroom area, she would probably be trapped anyway, because she had no doubt the man who pursued her wouldn't be stopped by the obstacle of a mere door.

Nor, she reminded herself bitterly, would he be stopped even if the room did change.

The hand dropped uselessly to her side, and she turned away from the hall.

Closer: *Amy* . . .

She glared at the room and its unrelenting black, demanding that it tell her its secret, tell her where her friends had gone.

But however it was illuminated, there were no reflections or distortions to provide her with a clue. And there were no answers.

Wrong, she corrected with an angry shake of her

head: there were real answers here, but she couldn't think of the right way to ask the right questions.

He had her so rattled, so upset, she couldn't think straight, rendering her incapable of making any solid connections between one thought and another. If there was only some way she could block out that voice; if there was only some way she could ignore him.

She had to stay rational no matter how insane the situation. Reason was the only way she would get out of this alive.

Closer: *Amy Lowell* . . .

Her hands bunched into frustrated fists, beating angrily at the air as she stared at the room intently. Somewhere in here she had missed something vital. She *had* to have missed something. But like the other areas of her nightmare, the single solid color only served to confuse her, blending the corners into invisibility, blending the walls into the floor and ceiling. Yet she had searched it all as best she could, and the only thing left was the mirror, and it sure wasn't the Looking Glass, and she sure wasn't Alice about to step through it.

She blinked slowly.

"That's nuts," she said.

Why not? she answered silently.

"No." Deliberately she looked away, and just as deliberately she looked back.

Why not?

Because it's nuts, that's why. Because it doesn't make any sense. Because it's . . . because it's . . .

Suddenly she pinched her arm hard enough to make her yelp and banish the confusion that threatened to overtake her.

All right, why, really, is that all so crazy? Why should something like a Looking Glass mirror be so completely out of the question when she had already seen a giant spider, a monster in a dungeon, and a virtually living thunderstorm? Why should she dismiss that idea out of hand when she had already closed one door and, without taking a step, showed up in another room, and not the one she had originally stepped into?

If that was all real . . .

She ran to it, fell to her knees, and after a cautious test to make sure neither the glass or frame composed some kind of trap, ready to shatter the moment she touched them, she rubbed the surface desperately with her left hand. Stinging grit dug into her palm like fine sandpaper, yet all she managed to do was shift the dirt around. So she pulled her right sleeve down until she could trap the end with the tips of her fingers, asked her mother to forgive her for ruining the new sweater, and rubbed again, just as hard.

A clear streak arced across the center, less than an inch wide.

She squinted at it, but could see nothing but a thin reflection of the black wall behind her.

Not permitting herself to feel defeat, she wiped the sleeve off on her jeans and tried again, widening the clean patch to two inches, then three, then into a ragged oval in the center wide enough for her to see her haggard face, and the curls that were plastered with sweat to her forehead.

She leaned back and scowled. The surface was slightly distorted, sending a dizzying ripple across her image from her chin to her ear. Her hand stretched out and pulled back. She was doing something wrong, but she couldn't figure out what it was.

A knuckle rapped the mirror again; the sleeve expanded the oval.

Amy, sweet Amy . . .

She shot a look at the doorway; he sounded as if he was at the bottom of the slope.

When she checked the mirror again, Spike stood behind her, waving to get her attention.

She cried out involuntarily and whirled around. "Spike, where—"

He wasn't there.

She rubbed her eyes hard with the backs of trembling hands, but he still wasn't there . . . until she looked back in the mirror.

A tiny swell of hope made her laugh giddily. She wasn't alone; she wasn't alone anymore. Even if he was in there, and she was still . . .

"How?" she asked.

He shook a finger at her, put it to his lips, then to his ear, then pointed at her while shaking his head quickly—he could hear her, perhaps, but she wouldn't be able to hear him. Then he leaned forward anxiously as if checking behind her, and beckoned urgently.

Cautiously she reached out toward the glass, almost expecting her hand to pass through it.

It didn't.

"How!" she demanded, hope too swiftly giving way to exasperation.

Becky appeared at his side, signaled to her to be patient, then scowled, said something to Spike, and finally held up one hand and turned it upside down. Two fingers extended downward, and she scissored them frantically.

"What?" She got to her feet, paced away and packed back. "I don't get it."

Becky repeated the mime, this time with Spike making a circle of his hands.

Amy understood instantly, and immediately shook her head helplessly. "I can't!" She bent over and tapped the glass to show them it was solid. "I can't!"

"Amy."

Coming slowly up the slope.

"Amy, are you ready?"

Spike and Becky's heads swiveled sharply as if they had heard him, their eyes widening with alarm. Then Spike took a step back and gestured for her to *come on, come on!* while Becky's cheeks turned red as she tried to yell instructions, instructions Amy couldn't hear.

But she did catch one word: *Run!*

"Amy."

Inhaling sharply, she looked to her right and saw a long shadow moving across the top of the slope.

His footsteps were clear now, like the constant beating of a heart.

With her hands out behind her, she backed away from the mirror, taking deep breaths, not taking her gaze off the image of her friends. She started when her fingers touched the wall, and the breathing came more quickly.

Then he stepped into the room.

"Amy," he chided. "Haven't you had enough?"

"Go away!" she yelled.

He closed his eyes and laughed.

That moment was all she needed—she launched herself off the wall and was at a dead run in a single stride.

Angrily he commanded her to stop.

Three feet from the wall, she stretched her arms out as if in a dive, leapt, and plunged headfirst into the mirror.

19

Despite Spike's clumsy attempt to catch her, she landed on her chest, her chin smacking the floor, momentarily stunning her. Air rushed from her lungs, and she rolled with a loud moan onto her side, doubling over and wheezing for a breath that didn't burn her lungs.

As the pain began to subside and her lungs started working again, she tried to crawl away, gasping that the man was right behind her. Hands fluttered over her arms and face, holding her, stroking her, until the terror bled away, and she realized that, for the moment at least, she was safe.

When she was finally able to sit up, feeling as if someone had taken a bat to her jaw, Spike knelt behind her to support her back, while Becky knelt in front, hands clenched, tears drenching her cheeks.

"We thought we'd lost you," she said.

Amy managed a tremulous smile. "Not . . . quite."
She massaged her chest and winced. "But almost."

"How do you feel?" Spike asked.

"Another one of those stupid questions?"

He shrugged with his eyebrows, then told her to
look around.

"Oh, God," she moaned, "where are we now?"

Though her vision was slightly blurred, she glanced
around the room she'd landed in, and didn't believe it.
She choked back a laugh and went up to her knees.

It was the dining room—the original dining room.
The windows were blocked, the table was still there,
and patterns of dust scattered across the floor.

Painfully she rose to her feet.

"No," Spike told her gently.

She stared in disbelief. "But—"

"But almost," Becky added excitedly. She pointed
across the foyer to the parlor. "No fireplace. It's the
only difference we can find."

Spike explained that they hadn't been here very
long, just enough to be fooled, and to crash when they
realized it wasn't the same place. That they were close,
however, he proved by switching on his flashlight—
the beam was practically normal. That's when Amy
noticed the room was quietly lighted. There were no
candles or lamps or lanterns or torches that she could
see; the air itself seemed to glow.

She propped herself wearily against the table and
stared at the mirror on the wall, a duplicate of the one
she had escaped through. Then she saw Jon sitting in
the corner. His eyes were closed, his breathing irregu-

lar. She went to him and placed her hand against his brow, and the heat of his fever touched her skin before she touched his.

"We were waiting for you," Spike said, "before we tried to find the last exit."

She shook her head. "You shouldn't have. He needs a hospital."

"We had to," he said softly. "We're buddies, remember? We weren't going to leave you."

A catch in her throat prevented her from speaking. Instead, she leaned closer, and whispered to Jon to hang in there just a little while longer. Then she stepped into the foyer and looked down the hall.

So close . . . and she wondered if she had the nerve to open that kitchen door.

"Hey," Becky said quietly.

She started forward.

"Amy, wait!"

The urgency in Becky's voice got her back in a hurry, her question unasked when she saw them staring at the mirror.

He was there.

He was smiling.

And as she watched, his face expanded to fill the glass, then spread over the frame, his torso and legs slipping out of the bottom.

Quickly they put the table between themselves and the man, and watched in fearful silence as his ghost-like form shimmered, and became solid.

"You've been very annoying, children," he scolded. He wasn't smiling. "Very annoying indeed."

"So?" Spike blustered, whipping out his wrench. "Let us go and we won't bother you anymore."

The man looked at the ceiling and smiled. "Oh, I doubt that, Oliver. I doubt that very much." He leveled his gaze at them. "I'm sorry to say, you'll have to be—"

"I know who you are!" Amy blurted.

"What are you talking about?" Becky whispered.

The man simply watched.

She didn't know why she hadn't thought of it before, because now she knew how they could get away.

She sidled toward the foot of the table, stopping the others from following with a short angry glance. "You're the house, aren't you," she said. "However this thing started, you're everything in here." She moved another step, and sensed Spike begin to move the other way. "You're that thing in the dungeon, and you were the wind and that lightning . . . and you were whatever chased Jon, too."

His smile broadened, baring perfect white teeth. He raised his gloved hands and applauded her without a sound. "Nicely done, Amy Lowell." The voice echoed. "I knew you wouldn't disappoint me in the end."

"You killed Dev's brother," she accused.

"Just part of the game," he said blandly. "Sometimes you win, sometimes you lose."

Fury made her chest tight. "That's a lie. You never lose."

He nodded. "Yes. But there's always that chance."

Suddenly Becky clambered on top of the table and glared down at him. "You probably pushed Jon down those stairs!" she shrieked.

Amy reached the end.

"Oh, go get down, child," the man said. "You're behaving like . . ." He laughed. "A child."

Amy dashed for the foyer.

"Stop!" he commanded.

She veered then toward Jon, dropped to her knees in front of him, and looked over her shoulder. "Let him go, okay? He's hurt, he needs help."

Becky shrieked wordlessly then, and the man glared, his patience clearly gone. As he took a step toward her, one hand out to grab her leg, Spike charged from the other side, the wrench held over his head like a battle-axe. Again distracted, he turned to his new annoyance, and that gave Amy all the time she needed.

She snatched the poker from Jon's lap, whirled as she stood, and swung it into the man's stomach, doubling him over and bringing him to his knees.

The Forever House *shifted*.

Amy stared into the parlor, then screamed, "Spike, do it!"

Spike stood over him as he bellowed in rage, hesitated, then brought the wrench down across his shoulders.

The Forever House *shifted*.

The man reached for the table for support, and Becky brought her heel down on his fingers just as Spike clubbed him again.

• • •

. . . *shifted*

"Yes!" Amy cried.

The room went dark, but not before she saw the fireplace appear in the parlor wall.

Becky turned on her flashlight and leapt to the floor, ran to the corner and, with Amy's help, brought Jon to his feet. He complained, but he moved as they half-walked, half-carried him into the hall.

"Hurry!" Spike yelled. "He's coming around."

He ran up behind them and, heedless of Jon's groans, picked up his legs. The three then rushed toward the kitchen, the beam of Becky's light darting ahead.

"You won't make it, children," a deep voice threatened.

Amy kicked the swinging door, and cried out silently when she saw the kitchen, and the moonlight slipping through the gaps in the windows' shutters.

Awkwardly they carried Jon across the floor, and she used her free hand to grab the knob.

The door was locked.

"No," she said.

The man laughed, and the house trembled.

They lay Jon down and attacked the door with poker and wrench, but succeeded only in making the man laugh harder. Amy turned and saw him standing in the foyer, face invisible, the white of his shirt glowing.

He took a step toward them.

She grabbed Spike's arm and dragged back. "Hurry," she urged. "We don't have any time."

Quickly she pointed, not wanting to speak aloud, and he caught the idea instantly. Then she stepped into the hall and put her hands on her hips, feeling anything but brave, but knowing it was the only thing she could do.

She said nothing.

The man's face drifted out of the shadows. He was smiling.

"You're very foolish," he said, moving toward her.

She lifted the poker to her shoulder.

"Foolish. Very foolish."

Behind her, Spike whispered, "Ready or not."

She wasn't.

But she charged the man anyway, screaming, swinging the poker so hard and so fast she nearly lost her balance.

He laughed and backed away, and Amy didn't think he could hear the battering noise behind her.

But he felt it.

She skidded to a halt as he suddenly straightened, eyes wide in astonishment.

Spike attacked the door's hinges again.

"No!" the man roared, but when he tried to run past her, Amy stepped aside and cracked the poker across his shins. He fell hard, sideways into the wall, and *shimmered* when Spike yelled, "Got one!"

In that instant, something, a *thing* took the man's place, until it *shimmered* again, and she saw a monstrous tiger with red eyes and black fangs, then a creature straight out of a madman's nightmare, then the man again, struggling to his knees.

She raced back to the kitchen, and saw Spike trying to split the bottom hinge. But the ancient iron wasn't as rusted through as had been the top one.

The man struggled to his feet, *shimmered,* but didn't change.

Amy yelled for Becky, and grabbed the edge of the door. When Becky joined her, the three of them pulled and twisted, forcing the rotten wood of the door's frame to slowly give way.

The man roared again and broke into a shambling run.

"Harder!" someone yelled.

The man stumbled and toppled into the wall, bellowed, *shimmered* . . .

The wood cracked, and the door fell into the hall.

Suddenly a powerful wind swept through the house, blinding them with dirt and dust, ripping wallpaper from its mooring, shattering what glass was left in the downstairs windows.

Covering their heads against the flying debris, they immediately ran to the back door, where Amy uttered a quick prayer, and pulled.

It opened.

And the wind slowly died.

20

Amy didn't remember very much for a while after that.

They carried Jon down the steps and into the yard, and Becky raced off to find a telephone to get some help. Their story was simple—they suspected Jon would be prowling around here tonight from things he had said in school, and they were right. They had found him injured and unconscious in the house, and brought him into the open.

Within minutes, an ambulance arrived, along with a patrol car and half the neighborhood. Amy did all the talking, calming the police before they got the wrong impression. Statements were taken, embarrassing praise was given for their quick thinking, and before they knew it, they were walking home.

"How did you know?" Spike finally asked.

"Flashlight," she answered, grinning. "I threw one at him, and just for a second, I had that same awful feeling like when the kitchen door first closed. Since he was the house, I figured if we could kill him or knock him out or something, the place would go back to normal."

"And the door," said Becky, "was the key, right? So we get rid of that and we get rid of that . . . maze, or whatever it was."

"Something like that."

They walked another block, grateful for the cool night air and the smell of the sea.

"Jon will be okay," she said to Becky when they reached her house. The ambulance attendant told him nothing seemed to be broken, and the fever and chills were simply a result of his body working to heal the damage.

Becky nodded gratefully, not daring to speak, and hurried up the walk, vanishing quickly inside.

Amy and Spike waited a few seconds, then turned and walked away, close to each other, bumping elbows now and then.

"You know," he said, squinting into the trees, "I don't think Dev was in there."

She agreed. The boy probably really had run away, but only because he wanted to find his brother. She hoped so, at least. Because after what they had done, the maze, and everything still in it, would be gone. Forever.

When they reached Oakwood Street, they paused on

the corner, staring up the block at the lights of her home.

"Nice trick with the quarter," she said.

"Hey," he said shyly.

"You kind of saved my life a little."

"Yeah, well . . . no big deal."

She closed one eye and glared. "My life is no big deal?"

"Now that's not what I meant," he said, suddenly flustered.

"It's what you said."

Before he could answer, she grabbed his arm, yanked him close, and kissed him.

It was . . . nice.

Especially when he blushed.

"Tomorrow, okay?" she said, stepping toward the house.

"Yeah." He gave her a quick wave. "Sure."

"Right."

"Okay."

She smiled. She grinned. She laughed and shook her head. Spike Amanti, longtime buddy, had suddenly become Spike Amanti, boyfriend. And it wasn't just because of what they had been through together.

"Hey, Amy?"

She turned, walking backward. He stood under a tree; she could barely see him for the shadows.

"He's not dead, is he?"

She hesitated, then shook her head.

He stepped into the street. "Just so I know." He

moved to the center. "We'll have to do something, huh?"

"Yep," she answered.

But he didn't hear her. He had already taken a step, a skip, and broken into a run that had him around the corner before she reached the front door.

But she wasn't worried about anyone reviving the Forever House.

She was, after all, Amy Lowell.

And even as she opened the door, she knew Amy Lowell had a plan.

*Please turn the page for
an exciting preview of the
next Taggard Point novel* . . .

Don't miss

SHAPES

available in May from Berkley Books

The fog is different in Taggard Point.

Every spring, every autumn, it rolls in from the sea like smoke from a silent fire, or rises from the Indian River, barely visible at all.

At least once a week it slips through town, hiding in the leaves, clinging to the light, brushing a cheek like the touch of a spider.

But whenever it comes, and wherever it comes from, there's never a warning.

Clear days before sunset will suddenly turn hazy; cloudy days at noon will suddenly turn gray.

At night you never see it coming at all.

It was the only thing Holly Lamand really disliked about the Point.

In the city she and her mother had left two years

before, the fog was usually romantic, like something out of an old movie where lovers meet and foghorns call and the sound of hoofbeats echoes off cobblestones.

In the Point, while it was rarely thick enough to blind, it was always enough to distort familiar landmarks and make the dark streets darker.

It also made walking home seem to take twice as long.

She shivered a little and turned away from the drugstore window, picked up her clipboard and red pencil, and went back to work.

Counting perfume bottles and lipsticks was not the most exciting thing to do on a Friday night. In fact, unless it was counting the holes in the acoustic-tile ceiling, she couldn't think of anything more boring.

She scowled at the inventory chart, scowled at the array of boxes and bottles on the shelves in front of her, glanced at her right at the front window, and sighed.

Out there, beyond the weak neon reach of Spielman's Drugs, somewhere in the fog, was a whole town, and she was pretty sure that everyone in it was either at the movies, at a party, or on their way to the movies or a party. They certainly weren't in here. And they hadn't been for over an hour. With less than thirty minutes to closing, she doubted anyone would be.

But would Mr. Spielman let her go early?

She snorted. Mr. Spielman wouldn't let her go early if the President was on the sidewalk, asking for her by name.

She dropped the clipboard on the display counter

behind her, and jumped at a muffled coughing in the back room, a familiar sound that made her feel instantly guilty. Mr. Spielman wasn't all that bad, not really; he just had different ideas about fun ways to spend weekend nights. At least he let her wear jeans to work; some of the girls she knew actually had to wear dresses and stockings.

She sighed again, picked up a neon-pink feather duster, and pretended the store needed a good cleaning. It didn't. It was about as crowded as something this small could get and still leave room for three aisles, but dust didn't dare show its face in here.

Fifteen minutes later she was done, including making sure all the merchandise was arranged neatly in the shelves, and the magazines, paperback books, and greeting cards were straight in their racks.

A glance at her watch—fifteen minutes more.

With her hands clasped loosely behind her back, she wandered up the center aisle. The store was at the southeast corner of Tidal Row and Marlen Street, its recessed doorway facing the intersection dimly lit by a single working streetlamp, hazed now by the fog.

It was only approaching eleven o'clock, yet there was no traffic. There seldom was at night, this close to the edge of town.

The hollow rattle of brass loops told her Mr. Spielman had left the back room, shoving aside the heavy black curtain that served as a door. She heard his raspy, labored breathing as he checked the cash register, checked her inventory list, and mumbled to himself.

"Miss Lamand?"

It was an old voice, cracked like portions of the shop's linoleum floor.

"Right here," she answered, turning with a smile.

He was short, stocky, never without his white pharmacist's jacket or his wire-rimmed glasses, often perched near the top of his nearly bald pate. He squinted. "You cleaned?"

"I sure did."

He nodded, and pulled at his nose. "You get paid today?"

She managed to hide a grin. "No, not tonight. Next week."

"Ah." He smiled as if the question had been a test. "You're a good girl, do you know that? A very good girl."

She had no answer, could only mutter her thanks.

He tapped the register thoughtfully with a finger and walked up to join her. She was pleased to see that his limp hadn't returned. Recently he had had treatment for what he laughingly called an "old war wound," and as the limp faded he actually seemed to grow taller.

"Quiet night," he said.

She nodded. "It's always quiet out here."

He chuckled, coughed, then shook his head and rapped the glass door lightly with his knuckles. "It's back, I see."

Holly felt uneasy at the way he said it. It was almost as if he were somehow glad. "I hope it doesn't get any worse, or I'll end up walking into the ocean."

"You know," he said quietly, "when I was boy in the

old country, this come all the time. From the mountains. It come into the villages and make them hidden. There were animals too. They follow the fog, use it to hunt. No wolves, they're gone a long time ago. Other things. Owls, wild cats and dogs." He laughed quickly. "They make everything very . . ." He looked up at her, frowning. "Spooky?"

"Absolutely," she agreed. "Really spooky."

He nodded. "Really spooky. Yes, it was. Things you thought you knew in the day are only shapes then. You never really know what they are when there are nights like this." The smile faded as he sniffed and rubbed the back of his neck. "Have you see Mrs. Emmers?"

Holly shook her head. Mrs. Emmers was a tiny woman in her early sixties, who didn't look strong enough to withstand a strong breeze; yet she had never missed an evening walking past the store, holding a leash at the other end of which were two German shepherds.

Two weeks ago, however, for reasons no one had yet been able to explain, the dogs had broken away from her near her home, howling and barking. Later that night, the police found them near the river. Someone had killed them.

According to rumor, it had not been a pleasant sight.

"I think," Mr. Spielman said, "I drop in to see her. She might like the company."

Holly agreed, then winked and suggested he bring her a box of candy.

The old man mock-scowled. "I go to talk, Miss Lamand, not marry the lady." His smile was brief.

"When I marry, I will pick someone young, and beautiful, and very rich." He laughed. "Like you, perhaps."

"Oh, sure," she said. "Right."

"But your mother is a doctor, yes? I thought all doctors in America were very rich."

Holly looked out at the haze around the streetlamp. "Not all of them, Mr. Spielman. Not all of them."

"Ah." He shrugged, and cleared his throat. "Well, I guess we might as well call it a day. What do you think? Do you think the thundering herds will come in at the last minute and make us both rich?"

She couldn't help a rueful laugh. "I don't think so."

He gestured sharply at the street in not-quite-feigned disgust. "Nah. Me, neither. The herds don't come anymore, do they?" His shoulders slumped as he looked out one more time before heading toward his office. "You go now, all right? Give my best to your dear mother. I'll turn out the lights, lock the door."

"Are you sure?" The last time that had happened, the lights had burned all night, and when she'd come in the next day, the front door had been unlocked. "I can wait to do it, really. It's only a couple of minutes."

"No, no, no," he insisted. He rounded the counter and held the curtain aside. "You go. I lock up." He shrugged. "Nothing else to do, is there?"

She wanted to say something, but he was already gone, the black cloth swaying, the brass loops clacking dully on their hollow brass rod. Nevertheless, she took her time fetching her denim jacket and purse, just in case. When he didn't return, she called a goodbye, flipped the OPEN sign to CLOSED, and ducked outside.

As she stood in the doorway, slipping on the jacket against the chill of the early May night, she shivered a little at the touch of the fog.

On nights like tonight, when it brushed over her face, it made her think of cobwebs.

Oh good, she thought with a sour grin; spook yourself, why not, before you even get started.

Not that Mr. Spielman hadn't helped, all that talk about the "old country," the mountain fog, and the animals that prowled through it.

Not to mention bringing up what had happened to that poor old lady's pets.

Still, as a boss he was okay. He had hired her when he really didn't need the help, and every so often gave her a generous bonus when she had done nothing special to deserve it. She had stopped protesting a long time ago; it only made him upset.

A car's horn sounded, quick and distant.

The three shops adjoining the drugstore were already closed; although she could see the glow of the main business district far to her left, she could make out no individual cars, no pedestrians, not even the traffic lights.

The fog, thin as it was, smeared it all.

It even muffled the hush of a breeze drifting aimlessly through the new leaves.

It sounded like someone whispering in her ear.

She hugged herself, but didn't move.

So what are you waiting for? she asked her pale reflection in the display window at her shoulder.

Her reflection, the ghost of a girl with dark auburn hair and wide green eyes, high cheeks and slightly pointed chin, shrugged.

Liar, she told it.

Dan; she was waiting for Dan.

The trouble was, he wasn't coming.

She stepped out to the curb.

A car hissed by, heading out of town, taillights flaring at her before they disappeared.

She had spent half the night fantasizing about his leaving Greta's party early, too miserable to stay without her at his side. A nice fantasy, but that's all it was, and she chided herself for acting like a lovesick jerk.

Fantasies only came true in the movies.

She trotted across the Row then, a double-wide boulevard that split the Point in half from the board-walk to the woodland that was its western border. Once on the other side, she paused, her head tilted slightly to one side.

Something had made a faint noise up the street, but she couldn't see very clearly.

Once again she thought about the German shep-herds, two animals that, despite their age, were large enough to handle anything short of a mountain lion.

Someone had killed them.

Someone, if the stories were only half true, had almost torn them apart with a butcher's knife or a cleaver.